Falling for
the Enemy

a Private Pleasures novel

Samanthe Beck

Entangled Publishing, LLC
2614 South Timberline Road
Suite 109
Fort Collins, CO 80525
Visit our website at www.entangledpublishing.com.

Brazen is an imprint of Entangled Publishing, LLC. For more information on our titles, visit www.brazenbooks.com.

Edited by Heather Howland and Sue Winegardner
Cover design by Heather Howland
Photography by iStock

Manufactured in the United States of America

First Edition December 2014

To Mom. When you said, "Nothing's shocked me yet," you didn't mean it as a challenge, but...

Chapter One

Holy crap, I'm going to die like a gnat, splattered against a windshield.

The thought blazed through Virginia Boca's mind while a pathetically unremarkable montage of her life flashed before her eyes. Twenty-eight years of sucking in the country air of Bluelick, Kentucky was about to come to a gruesome end thanks to that reckless little shithead, Justin Buchanan, and the stupid red Mustang his idiot father bought him last year for his sixteenth birthday. Worse, after running her down in the street like a dog, Justin would probably walk away with a slap on his wrist, because his idiot father also happened to be mayor. And without her around to throw her hat into the ring, Tom Buchanan would win re-election next month without breaking a sweat.

The steel death machine barreled down on her, so close she could see Justin through the windshield, texting away while speeding along Main Street. A scream slammed into her frozen vocal cords, but she could no more free the noise than she could change direction in midair. She'd already passed the point of no return on the journey from sidewalk to the crosswalk, and now momentum held her prisoner.

Time slowed and stretched as the Mustang neared. Justin looked up. Their eyes met. His went wide and filled with the kind of terror that came from confronting a math problem along the lines of, "How many feet does it take to stop a two-ton car traveling at sixty miles per hour?" and realizing the answer was more than he had.

Ginny closed her eyes—not so much because she accepted her fate, but because she preferred not to be there for it—and braced her body for a brutal kick-off into the hereafter.

An arm banded around her middle and yanked her backwards so fast she lost what she'd assumed would be her last breath. Displaced air from the speeding car buffeted her, but nothing more. She opened her eyes. Despite the black dots dancing around the perimeter of her vision, she managed to see the Mustang disappear down Main without a single flash of brake lights.

Shithead.

She might have indulged in a longer, more inventive rant, except the dancing black dots made her dizzy and a little queasy. She blinked fast, trying to clear them, but the stubborn things merged together to limit her vision to twin tunnels while the rest of her body turned as weightless as a helium balloon. Maybe Justin had hit her after all, and this was what death felt like? If so, the dark tunnels were even more troubling. Wasn't there supposed to be a light to float into? Lord knew she wasn't a saint. She'd fallen a bit short of chaste at times, and yes, she gossiped more than she should, but she'd recently vowed to mend her ways and do something meaningful with her life. Where the hell was…er, scratch that…where in *heaven's* name was her light?

Strong arms kept her tethered in place and a low voice murmured, "You're okay."

The words vibrated in her ear, echoed around in her foggy head, and then surged down her spine, forcing her nervous system into a shaking, stuttering re-boot. Her brain attempted a physical inventory and picked up some unsettling stimuli—whipcord taut thighs braced to support her far better than her own trembling legs, a sloping wall of hard abs along her back, and a warm, wide chest pressed against her like a shield.

Her neck muscles took a time out, and the back of her head connected with a well-developed pectoral, then lolled to the side and her cheek settled against the muscular cushion. A strong, rapid heartbeat pounded under her ear, and his rough breath fanned her temple. Both told her she and Justin weren't the only ones hopped up on adrenalin from their near-fatal game of car versus pedestrian. She stood there shivering while he did all the work—kept her from sinking to the sidewalk while somehow managing to slow his breathing and his heart rate.

Her breath and heartbeat played follow-the-leader and synched up with his, and her awareness of every plane and angle of the unquestionably male body behind her heightened. She'd never had a premonition in her life, and didn't particularly believe in them, but apparently a near-death experience coupled with a months-long sex hiatus brought about heretofore undiscovered powers, because a vivid image filled her mind. Her, naked and backed up against her guardian angel while he ran his big, sure hands down her sides and clasped her hips. She arched her back, groaned, and—

His answering groan pulled her back to the here and now—and to the unmistakable ridge burning a brand along the seam of her jeans. *Get ahold of yourself, Ginny. You don't say "Thank you for the save" by rubbing yourself all over a stranger.* She lowered her eyes and saw her hands clamped around strong, tanned forearms. Her fingernails dug into his skin as if her life still depended on him.

Release death grip now. At the same time she loosened her hold, his arms tightened fractionally around her, keeping her in place. His jaw brushed her ear. He exhaled slowly, then released her, and stepped away. The warm June evening didn't stop a final shiver from skipping up her spine at the sudden absence of his body heat.

She turned to face her rescuer and experienced a jolt of…inevitability. She didn't *know* him, but she recognized him. Recognized his mass of overgrown dark hair, stubbly jaw, and deep, brown, impenetrable eyes. She'd seen him around town several times over the last few weeks, always solitary, always silent, but something in the way he carried his tall, hard-packed frame hinted at coiled energy beneath his cool, relaxed surface. Solitary and silent were about as far from her type as a guy could get, but this man worked every erogenous zone in her body with nothing but his brooding stare.

Gossip abounded about his identity, and as the owner of the busiest hair salon in town, she heard every word of it. She didn't have a clue if any of the reports contained a kernel of truth, but his dangerous, almost feral appearance had inspired her friend Melody to dub him "Wolverine."

Before she could ask him his name, he turned and...*for God's sake*...started walking away.

"Wait!" she called to his retreating back. He didn't slow, so she yelled, "Thank you."

He shrugged his broad shoulders in the universal *no worries* gesture.

"Hey!" She waited until he craned his neck around and looked at her. Then she pointed to the entrance of her salon. "I owe you a haircut."

His hand came up in a casual salute, and that's all the acknowledgment she got. He made a right at the end of the block and disappeared around the corner.

Well, hell. Her system revved with the impulse to chase him down, but a quick glance at her watch nixed the notion. She was already late to meet Melody at Rawley's Pub. Damn it, she had to walk away from tonight's encounter with her curiosity—not to mention a few other things—unsatisfied.

• • •

Shaun Buchanan climbed behind the wheel of his stripped-down Wrangler, started the engine, and fought the urge to head straight out of town and keep going until he drove clean off the continent. The sexy little redhead might consider his presence outside her salon tonight a lucky coincidence, but he knew better. For weeks now he'd been finding excuses to pass by at the end of the day, blend into the shadows like a ghost, and watch as she talked and joked with her last customers.

An unsettling habit, considering "ghost" was an apt description of him these days, and that's just how he wanted it. He intended to stay on the untethered fringe, not get drawn in. She, on the other hand...everything about her drew people in. Her salon buzzed with activity most of the day. A steady stream of clients overlapped, lingered, and chatted while the auburn-haired beauty worked her magic. She had the energy and personality to match her business. She was a talker, and a toucher, adept at putting people at ease— though "at ease" definitely didn't describe him after having her slender curves locked against him during their brief-but-intense encounter. Her sultry, slightly husky voice lingered in his ears, but in his imagination she was calling out a grateful "thank you" for entirely different reasons.

If it was only his pent-up libido pulling him in, he wouldn't find the situation so troubling. But it went deeper. She radiated purpose and vitality—two qualities sadly lacking in his life at the moment—and they attracted him at the same time he told himself to steer clear.

He put the Jeep in gear and took the familiar route toward Riverview Road and the big, stately homes of Bluelick's bluebloods. He had zero capacity for getting involved. Not with the community, or his messed-up family, and certainly not a hot redhead with twinkling green eyes and a quick mouth.

Thanks to Justin, family involvement couldn't be avoided tonight, but the rest of it? Hell, yes. He maneuvered his Jeep into the circular cobblestone driveway of the largest house on a street of large homes, and pulled in behind the red Mustang parked haphazardly at the apex. A few strides brought him to the white doors of the colonial he'd called home for the first twelve years of his life. He'd barely set foot in the place over the next seventeen, but he walked in as if he owned it.

Justin stood in the entryway, screwing around on his phone. He looked up when Shaun strolled toward him.

"What?"

The single word dripped with attitude. Shaun ignored the tone. "Where's Dad?"

Justin shrugged and returned his attention to his phone. "Out to dinner with fuck-me-up-the-ass Barbie."

By that lovely endearment, he assumed Justin referred to the third and latest in the line of Mrs. Tom Buchanans— twenty-three-year-old former cocktail waitress Brandi something-or-other, who had hastened the inevitable split between their father and Justin's mom. Fidelity wasn't Tom's strong suit, and he had two ex-wives to prove it. Equally apparent, there was no love lost between Justin and Brandi.

"Better watch your mouth, unless you want to spend your senior year at a military academy in Savannah."

His brother looked up and smirked. "Fuck that shit. I'll go live with my mom."

Not likely, based on what he knew of Justin's mom, and he suspected her only son realized as much. Still, he didn't bother correcting the statement. Justin's custody options were not his concern. He held out his hand for the phone. "Can I see that for a sec?"

The teen gave him an irritated look but handed it over. "It's an iPhone, dumbass. Didn't they have those in the SEALs?"

He dropped the sleek device to the floor and stomped it under his heel. The screen shattered.

"Hey, you freak, what the fuck—?"

"Now it's a piece of garbage. If I see you speeding through town again, the car is my next target. Got that, *dumbass*?"

"You're bat-shit crazy. I'm telling Dad."

"Go ahead. Be sure to mention the part where you almost killed someone while you were texting and driving. Bet he buys you a new phone right about the time hell freezes over."

Dark eyes disconcertingly similar to his own burned with pure, unadulterated hate, and the kid's hands tightened into fists. Part of him hoped his little brother would go ahead and take a swing, because as far as he could tell the kid needed an ass-kicking, but dishing one out meant sticking around for a bunch of physical and emotional cleanup he preferred to avoid. So he dished out his version of cautionary advice instead. "Thinking about banging heads with me? Think about this. I'm taller, I'm heavier, and I'm trained to drop a guy twice your size. I can grind you under my boot just like this"—he kicked the battered phone so it slid to a stop by the toe of Justin's two-hundred-dollar athletic shoes—"without breaking stride."

The anger had to go somewhere, so Justin swung his foot and kicked the phone into the baseboard, where it landed with a thud and a shower of parts. "You suck." He turned and stormed up the central staircase. "Go back to Afghanistan, or Pakistan, or whatever shithole you came from, and stay there this time."

"Aw, you've hurt my feelings." Petty, but for some reason he couldn't resist having the last word. He was dead tired, still pissed, and, frankly, they'd never been close. He'd been ten when his parents had split. With the ink barely dry on the divorce decree, Tom had turned around and married Monica. She'd been such a bitch on wheels Shaun had gladly escaped to military school a couple years later when Justin came along.

A combination of choice and circumstances—including four years at Annapolis and six years with the SEALs—had kept him away pretty consistently since then. Despite the lack of brotherly bonds, he harbored some sympathy for the kid. Or at least not complete apathy, he silently corrected as he returned to his car. Monica had moved to Atlanta without a backward glance. According to their father, she couldn't be bothered to do more than send an occasional text to Justin.

He steered the car back the way he'd come and thought about the other half of the parental equation—their father. Tom Buchanan loved his sons…in his own distracted, dysfunctional way. His parenting technique swung between benign neglect and attempts to overcompensate for his lack of attention by doing favors and purchasing affection. No surprise Justin had turned out spoiled and self-centered. Life with Mommy and Daddy had taught him to put his needs and desires first, or nobody would. *Not your problem,* a weary voice in his head interjected. *You've got plenty of your own.*

A left turn onto Main brought the salon into sight for the second time, and a few personal needs and desires pushed to the forefront of his mind. They centered around the woman he'd held in his arms less than an hour ago, her body pressed so close he could still feel the imprint of tight, toned curves in some very key places. The citrus-y scent of her perfume, or shampoo, or whatever it was, still flirted with his senses—something as distinct and teasingly sexy as the rest of her.

Her soft, shuddery moan reverberated in his memory and fueled all sorts of highly entertaining and incredibly inadvisable thoughts.

Her words replayed in his brain as he drove past the shop. *I owe you a haircut.*

Without meaning to, he glanced at his reflection in the rearview mirror. Dark hair fell across his forehead, nearly to his eyes. His pulse kicked up at the thought of taking her up on her offer.

If he was smart, he'd go to Lexington for a haircut. Or Darfur. Or Mars. Any of those would be less risky. Hell, he'd cut it himself. He was taking care of all his other personal needs these days. Why break tradition? Especially not with a sultry salon owner he could too easily imagine giving him much more than a trim.

Chapter Two

Ginny flipped her sign to CLOSED and pulled the string to lower the bamboo blinds shielding the large, street-facing window of her salon. A glance through the glass sent a prickling sensation down her bare arms as tiny hairs stood at attention. There he was—Wolverine—standing at the curb, about to enter the crosswalk. Dusk had fallen in the time necessary to turn dark-haired Dilly Hill into a summer blonde, but the waning light didn't matter. Nor did the fact that he wasn't facing her. She recognized him by sheer size, shape, and the disciplined stillness with which he held himself.

He'd invaded her subconscious every night in the weeks since he'd saved her ass, interrupting her ordinary fare of "winning the lottery" and "forgetting to study for the Geometry final" dreams with erotic, naked adventures. The kind of adventures she awoke from all itchy and achy…and alone. She and her pillow had gotten unusually close, because a woman on a self-imposed sex hiatus had to take matters into her own hands. Talented as they were, her hands couldn't conjure up the heat and tension of his body pressed against hers. They couldn't recreate the thump of his heart or the weight of his strong arms wrapped around her. Imagination only got her so far, and she was quickly learning when it came to certain things, "so far" wasn't nearly far enough.

Without thinking, she rapped the glass with her knuckle. If the sudden noise startled him, he controlled all outward tells. No jolt. No searching around for the source of the sound. He simply turned his head and zeroed in on her like he'd sensed her presence the entire time. She hurried to the door and pushed it open. "What are you doing right now?"

His clothes suggested nothing fancy. Wash-faded jeans showed off long, powerful legs and molded to an indecently perfect ass, while the plain, black T-shirt fit snug over biceps she wanted to sink her teeth into. Clearly not a man headed out for a night on the town, but he stayed silent for long enough to make her wonder if he planned to answer. She arched a brow and leaned against the door, sending him a silent "I can keep this stand-off going all night" message. She flexed her toes inside her unlaced, low-top Chucks and briefly wished for heels to lend her some height and authority, but spending all day on her feet had taught her to wear comfy shoes on the job. She'd just have to think tall and channel authority.

Maybe it worked, or maybe he was just the world's slowest conversationalist, but he replied, "Nothing."

His shuttered expression offered no nuance to the single-word response. Ditto for his body language—not so much as a head shake. Fine and dandy. Let him do his badass, stoic thing. It took more than that to intimidate her. "You saved my life. The least I can do is give you a shave and a haircut."

The stoic expression slipped and his dark eyes became a war zone of conflicting emotions. Desire, (she hadn't been on her hiatus so long she didn't recognize that particular look), reluctance, and something indefinable she might have called panic on anyone else. He looked away, rasped his palm over his whiskered jaw, and when he faced her again, he had his give-nothing-away look firmly in place. "Okay. Thank you."

Three words in a row. New record. "No, no. This is me thanking you," she shot back as she held the door open with one arm and stepped aside to allow him to enter. His shoulder brushed against her chest when he squeezed past. The completely innocent contact sent not-so-innocent heat zinging through her, firing up nerve endings until even her toes tingled. For one disorienting moment she flashed back to the memory of having his tall, sturdy frame supporting her. He turned to her and cocked a brow, as if awaiting instructions, but a distinctly knowing look lurked in his eyes. Heat reversed course and stormed into her face.

Hold the phones, girl, you *make people blush, not vice versa.*

"Have—" Geez, was that crackling noise her voice? She cleared her throat and tried again. "Have a seat there." She pointed through her small lobby to the adjustable-height swivel chair in front of her workstation. "I'll be right over."

He nodded and walked to the chair. She flicked on more lights and finished lowering the blinds. It might have been smarter to leave them up, because her little salon suddenly seemed even smaller, but it was dark outside and she disliked working in a fishbowl.

To combat the intimacy, she detoured to the counter separating the waiting area from the main salon and turned on the radio. Bruno Mars filled the silence, crooning about sex and paradise. So much better. She turned the volume low and headed to the rinse sink at the back of her salon. Once there, she turned on the hot water and pulled a hand towel from the stack on the shelf beside the sink. Out of the corner of her eye she watched him stare at his reflection in her workstation mirror. No. Correction. He tracked *her* movements in the mirror. As she tested the temperature of the water, she became intensely aware of the band of ex-posed skin below the hem of her red tank top and above the hip-riding waist of her denim skirt. Was she flashing him a whale-tail? Awesome. She thrust the towel into the wa-ter. Nothing screamed "classy" like the back of her thong peeking out over the top of her skirt. She turned off the tap, tugged her tank down, and wrung the excess water from the towel. "I don't think we've officially met. I'm Ginny."

"Short for Jennifer?"

With the hot towel bundled to retain heat, she walked to the chair and met his eyes in the mirror. "Short for Virginia, but everybody calls me Ginny."

Silence. She unfurled the steaming towel and held the corners by her fingertips to let it cool. "This is where you say, 'Nice to meet you Ginny, I'm…state your name here.'"

The corner of his mouth tipped up in the slightest of smiles. "Shaun."

"Lovely to meet you. Got a last name, Shaun?" She used the foot pedal to lower the chair a few inches, and then tipped it back slightly.

"It's a mouthful." Her attention drifted to his mouth,

and in her mind she heard him add, *like everything about me*. Instead, he said, "Just call me Shaun."

She puffed out a breath and pressed her lips together to calm the suddenly hyperactive nerve endings there. "All righty then. Lean your head back…perfect," she said when he did as she asked. She draped the towel over his face. "Let me know if this is too hot."

An indistinct murmur served as his reply. She took it as a no, and pulled a clean cape from a lower workstation drawer. A practiced flick of her wrists unfurled it over him. She secured it behind his neck, and then got busy whipping shave cream into a thick lather with her brush. When that was done, she used her palms to pat the towel against his cheeks for another moment, and then removed it and tossed it into the bin beneath the rolling cart parked next to her workstation. She eyed him in the mirror and brought her hands up to test his whiskers. Probably several days of growth, but not enough to warrant trimming with scissors first. Foam and a good, sharp razor would do the job.

Using the wide, badger fur shaving brush, she painted his throat, jaw, chin and cheeks with a layer of lather while considering conversation starters. Bluelick's most mysterious new face sat in her chair. She didn't intend to waste a golden opportunity to get the scoop on him. "Are you in town for business or pleasure?"

"Some of both."

She put the brush and bowl on the counter and opened a drawer. "What kind of business?" The shiny silver shield of her straight razor winked from the neatly arranged selection of grooming tools. She took it out and pushed the drawer closed with her hip, and then stepped behind him again. His eyes latched onto the razor and stayed there as she opened it. She wouldn't say he looked nervous, but he looked… cautious.

"Serious blade."

"Five-eighths inch, full hollow, carbon steel straight razor. You'll get a close shave."

"And then some," he muttered under his breath. To her he said, "You've done this before, right?"

Now she resisted the temptation to grin. "Please. I'm a licensed professional. Sit back. Relax. You're in good hands." She leaned in, tipped his chin up and placed the blade against his throat. Because the position put her mouth close to his ear, she modulated her voice and repeated her question. "What kind of business brings you to Bluelick?"

Her eyes found his in the mirror. He waited until she'd swept the blade from his Adam's apple to his chin before responding. "The boring kind. Nothing worth talking about."

Man, this guy was a tough nut. She cleaned the razor and positioned it for another pass. "You sell yourself short, Shaun. Bluelick's a small town. A new face creates a big stir around these parts." The next pass revealed another swath of smooth, sun-bronzed skin. Apparently a scruffy jaw wasn't his normal look.

His mouth twisted into the phantom smile again. "Has the rumor mill been grinding away on me?"

She found herself returning the smile. He knew a thing or two about small towns. "Hell, yes. You're the biggest mystery to hit Bluelick since someone set fire to a bag of dog poop and left it on Mr. Cranston's porch. Theories abound," she added as she cleared another path along his throat.

"I'm glad to know I rate right up there with dog crap.

Let's hear them."

"Well, I can't claim to know every single one."

"*You* sell yourself short, Virginia," he drawled. "I'll bet you hear everything. Something tells me people open up to you."

"Ginny," she automatically corrected, though aside from her name, he'd gotten everything else right. People did tend to open up to her. But the same bout of self-improvement that had inspired her currently inconvenient sex hiatus had given rise to her vow to stop spreading gossip. She couldn't necessarily help hearing things—she did own a beauty shop, after all—but she could resist the temptation to pass the stories along. No more talking behind people's backs. Then again, did it count as talking behind a person's back if the person she was talking to happened to be the subject of the rumor? Seemed like a legitimate loophole. Plus, she really wanted to know his story.

"I'll give you the top three," she said, working the razor over his jaw. A strong, masculine jaw. She tamped down on a wicked impulse to run her lips along the chiseled angle. "So long as you tell me if any of them are close to the truth."

He waited until she lifted the razor off his skin, and then slowly nodded, never breaking eye contact. For one wild moment she imagined he'd read her dirty mind and given her the go-ahead to put her mouth on him, but then reason kicked in.

"Okay. Um…" She rifled through her mental files for the most plausible backstory while sliding the razor along his cheek. "You're running from a checkered past, lying low in our backwater town while searching for redemption."

A low, rusty laugh rumbled up from his chest.

"Not so much?" she guessed.

"What else have you got?"

"Let's see." She finished his other cheek and came around front to shave his upper lip. "Some say you're one of those off-the-grid, lone-wolf types, bunkered in a cabin outside of town."

A series of short, careful passes with the razor completed the shave. She straightened.

"Jesus, a little facial hair really freaks you people out. I notice a distinctly sinister theme to these theories."

She couldn't help but laugh at his mildly offended tone. Using a clean towel, she wiped away the remaining flecks of shaving cream from his skin and inspected her handiwork… and nature's. Mercy, what a face. High, slightly sloping forehead, straight nose, cheekbones only God could have sculpted, and lips so perfectly kissable there ought to have been a law against hiding them beneath overgrown facial hair. They parted as her fingertip traced his philtrum. Belatedly, she realized she'd advanced from checking the closeness of his shave to something else entirely.

She pulled her hand back and cleared her throat. "You look a little less sinister now, don't you think?"

His eyes stayed on hers as he ran his palm over the lower half of his face. "I don't know about that, but I'm definitely smoother. Thanks."

Yet no less lethal, although without the shield of whiskers she could see fatigue dragging at the edges of his mouth. The shadows around his eyes looked more pronounced, too— less mysterious than plain old tired. Something in those eyes pulled at her. Something familiar. She couldn't place it, but she couldn't seem to look away either.

"What's the last theory?" he prompted.

"Huh? Oh, ah, I guess this one's kind of sinister, too. You're the long-lost, black-sheep son of a prominent local family."

A muscle clenched in his jaw an instant before he grinned and shook his head. "Very dramatic."

Despite the offhand comment, she sensed some new tension in him. "Remember our deal." She took a clean comb and scissors from the second drawer of her workstation and stepped behind him. "Any of them close to accurate?"

He hesitated for a moment and then shrugged. "Yes."

"Really?" Surprise had her lowering the comb. "Which one?"

"Sorry, that information isn't part of our deal. I agreed to tell you if any of them were close to accurate. I've done that."

"Oh, please. Don't mince my words. You know what I meant."

"Yes," he conceded, again without offering more.

She raised her scissors and snipped the air. "You sure you're not the barber? You're awfully good at splitting hairs."

"That's how us reclusive, black-sheep, redemption-seekers roll."

She gave him a long, patient stare…the one most people took as permission to unload their troubles, complaints or frustrations, but it bounced right off him. Talk about frustrating. "Whatever. How do you want your hair cut? Be very specific, because I wouldn't want to give you less than you expected."

He laughed off her jab. "I can honestly say I don't give a shit what you do to my hair. If it makes you happy, you can shave me bald."

"Don't tempt me." She saw no point in hiding the irritation in her voice—he'd baited her, and he knew it—but shame on her for being so damn easy to bait. Irritated or not, she wouldn't scalp him. Every single person who sat in her chair became a walking, talking advertisement for her business, and she took her business seriously. Additionally, she was poised to kick off her mayoral campaign tomorrow. Why give people a reason to doubt her judgment?

She narrowed her eyes and finger-combed his hair, trying to decide what she wanted to do with him...er...his hair.

Thick, dark brown strands shot with sun-burnished highlights sifted through her fingers. Great body. Nice wave. The kind of natural bounty God sometimes wasted on a man who "didn't give a shit" about his hair, while women forked over a couple hundred bucks every six-to-eight weeks for the exact same effect.

"Are you giving me the silent treatment, Virginia?" His question came out a little fuzzy around the edges. Not surprising. He'd come in the door tired, and now she was fiddling with his hair, relaxing him even more.

"Ginny," she corrected again. "Nobody calls me Virginia. It's too"—she wrinkled her nose and searched for the word—"virginal."

"It suits you."

"Ha. I can assure you I haven't been a virgin for a long time."

"You are, by one important standard."

"Oh, yeah?" She combed his hair with her fingers again. "How do you reckon?"

"You haven't had sex with me."

"Oh." *Oh? That's the best comeback you can manage?*

This time, thanks to the mirror, she got to enjoy not just the sensation of her face heating like an oven, but also the sight of pink staining her cheeks—just like a flustered virgin, for God's sake. Redheads were not meant to blush, and he'd pulled two out of her this evening. His satisfied smile suggested he knew he'd thrown her off her game. She snapped her mouth closed and concentrated on his hair.

"More silent treatment?"

She stopped messing with his hair and stared him down in the mirror. "I got the impression you didn't like to talk, sugar."

"Sugar?"

"Sorry, is that not what you like to be called? How rude of me."

He ignored the jibe. "*You* like to talk." In response to her unspoken question he added, "I've passed by a time or two. You're always chatting with clients while you work. Don't change on my account. I like listening to you. There's something very relaxing about your voice."

The admission softened her. She ran her fingernails lightly over his scalp, and searched for a topic. Thing was, monologues weren't her specialty. Normally she took her conversational cues from the client. She listened, responded with interest, and considered it part of the job of making the person in her chair feel comfortable. She picked up her spray bottle, pumped a few spritzes of water onto his hair and got to work with her comb. "What do you want me to talk about?"

"Anything…Whatever you were talking about with your last customer."

She thought back to her conversation with fifteen-year-old Dilly, which now seemed like a lifetime ago. "Okay." She started to snip. "We had a lengthy discussion about which member of One Direction is cutest. Dilly thought Harry. I'm more of a Zayn fan myself. And you?"

"I find it impossible to choose."

She grinned. "I know. They're all so adorbs." Her breast brushed his shoulder as she trimmed around his ear, and heat simmered through her at the brief contact. Her eyes darted to the mirror, found his, and registered the awareness in their depths. She cleared her throat and soldiered on. "I have to admit, I sometimes get Liam and Niall mixed up. I hope that doesn't shock you. Dilly practically swallowed her tongue when I told her I had a hard time telling them apart." She got into the rhythm as she spoke…comb, lift a section of hair, snip.

"God forbid," he murmured.

"She set me straight." A quick look up confirmed his eyelids had started to droop. She deliberately slowed her movements. If the haircut didn't send him off into dreamland, the conversation probably would. "Apparently Niall is a real blond, and kind of a goofball, which is, and I quote, 'totally obvious in every picture because there's this devilish glint in his eyes.' Liam, on the other hand, is a brunette with occasional blond streaks, and, according to Dilly, 'way more soulful and serious.'"

She glanced at the mirror again and smiled. Shaun's closed eyes and deep, even breaths declared him somewhat less enthusiastic a 1D fan than her previous client, who could have talked about the band for hours. Since there was nowhere particular she had to be, she took her time with the haircut and let him sleep. Why waste the opportunity to observe him unawares and appreciate his masculine beauty?

He looked younger, all clean shaven, freshly trimmed and combed. Younger and...familiar. The shape of his chin, the wing of his brows, triggered the odd, déjà vu feeling again. She stood stock still, staring at him as some memory danced along the perimeter of her consciousness, but it faded like a mirage as soon as she tried to pull it into focus.

Damn it, who *was* this guy? Impatient with herself, she gathered up her tools and set about putting things away. She removed the cape and shook it out, but he barely stirred. He snoozed with the same quiet containment he radiated when awake. Her trip to the supply closet for her broom and dust-pan went unnoticed, but on her way back to the workstation she heard him moan—a flat, reluctant sound escaping from the depths of a dream. Not a fleeting noise though. It increased in volume and urgency as she approached the chair, and the haunted, hopeless tone sent a shiver down her spine. Then his whole body jerked, and she nearly choked on her own startled scream.

Enough. She propped the broom against the wall and crouched down in front of him. "Hey," she said gently, not wanting to startle him, but determined to coax him away from whatever nightmare had sunk its claws into him. His moaning stopped, but his breathing turned choppy and a bead of sweat trickled down his temple. Without thinking, she reached up to wipe it away.

As soon as her fingertips brushed his skin his eyes popped open. Hard hands clamped around her upper arms. The room spun, but before she could utter a single cry of alarm, she was face-first against the mirror, trapped by his weight and his arms banded around her.

She swallowed hard, drew in a breath, and called, "Shaun!"

Chapter Three

Congratulations, you've finally had a psychotic break. Just as quickly as the unhelpful thought formed, he pushed it away. This was a dream. A bad one, mixed with flashbacks to make it extra nasty. Except…something wasn't right. An out-of-place, citrus-y smell didn't mesh with the all-too-familiar flashes of darkness, rubble, and some other horrific crap his mind refused to acknowledge. A voice called to him. Too high-pitched and feminine to belong to one of the other SEALs on the strike team, and laced with urgency—which in and of itself was not necessarily wrong, considering their target and what had gone down—but wrong because *this* voice called him by name.

Wake the fuck up. Now. He forced the word "Stop" from his tight, dry throat, and used the sound of his own voice to wrench himself out of the nightmare, and into…*oh shit*.

Adrenalin originally activated by the dream continued pouring into his overcharged system, even as he realized he had Virginia trapped between his body and the mirror, restrained in a bear-hug, with his forearm wedged against her soft breasts and a hard-on of undisguisable proportions prodding her backside. He immediately released her, stepped back, and waited for her fist to connect with his face, or her foot with his balls, or whatever else she dished out, because he definitely had it coming. She turned to face him, staring up at him with wide, cautious eyes.

"Sorry," he said lamely into the yawning silence. Heat crawled up his neck. His sleep problems usually took the form of insomnia, but on rare occasions he sleepwalked. He'd woken up in his closet once, the kitchen a few times, and in the garage once, which had been inspiration enough to flush the last of the sleeping pills his doctor had prescribed. Up until now he'd figured he'd flushed the sleepwalking as well, but tonight took the prize. He'd never laid a hand on anybody before. Of course, he'd been bedding down alone for the past several months, too tired and, frankly, too screwed up for company. *Way too screwed up.* He opened his mouth—to say what, he wasn't sure—but she interrupted him.

"Sugar, if you're not happy with your haircut, all you have to do is say so."

He caught the glint in those clear, green eyes. "Not funny."

"Oh, come on. It is kind of funny, when you think about it." She straightened her top. He ordered his eyes forward but they went AWOL and dropped to her chest. The skin on the inside of his forearms prickled with the phantom sensation of her rigid nipples poking him. His cock throbbed hard enough to have him biting back a groan. He had to get out of there. Now.

"Besides," she said, and smoothed her hands over her

short denim skirt in an unconscious gesture designed to kill him, "you were having a bad dream. You didn't jump me on purpose. No harm, no foul…" She looked up at him and trailed off, her eyes wide. He knew then and there all the desire surging through him showed on his face.

Retreat. But he didn't. He reached up and touched the small red mark riding high across her cheekbone—a souvenir from the mirror. Her skin felt like warm silk. "What would you have done?"

Her eyes were round and all pupils. "What would I have done if…what?"

"If I'd jumped you on purpose?"

He honestly didn't know who moved first, but in the next heartbeat they were on each other. Mouths fused. Hands grasping. He pulled her in closer and somehow ended up with her legs around his waist and her smooth, round handful of an ass right there in his palm. He squeezed. She moaned and tried to crawl under his shirt.

He tangled fingers into her hair, tugged her head back, and recaptured her mouth. Her kiss was as tantalizing and vital as the rest of her, and made him want to taste her everywhere—to consume all the heat and energy she offered. He moved his hand from her hair to the back of her neck in some primitive strategy to foreclose any escape route, and deepened the kiss, plunging his tongue into the sweet recess of her mouth with more hunger than finesse. She moaned again and raked her fingernails along his spine, setting off tiny bolts of lightning everywhere she touched.

Uncensored, unsupervised lust tore through him. Desperate to feed it, he sank his teeth into her lip and tightened his grip on her ass. She squirmed against him with such force he suddenly worried it stemmed more from agitation than pleasure.

He pulled back. "Fuck, I'm—"

No apology necessary. She yanked him back and took hard, fast little bites out of his lips while she worked his shirt up his chest. They wrestled his arms free, and then she swept it over his head, dragging some of his hair along with it.

"Sorry...I'm not usually...so grabby, but..."

"I don't care," he managed when she ran her lips over his chin. Her fingernail etched a trail across his chest. He knew without looking she traced the gothic script letters tattooed there. *The only easy day was yesterday.*

Over the last seven months the sentiment had never felt truer, except right here, right now, because falling into Virginia felt easier than breathing—and just as critical. He slid his hand from the back of her neck around to her throat, over her collarbone and down the inviting slope of her chest.

A shiver racked her when he squeezed her breast. Her legs tightened around his hips. "It's just lately...I've been on...this...sex hiatus."

Him, too, now that he thought about it, but then thought got more difficult because her soft, quick lips scorched a path from his chin to his earlobe, and then she latched on and sucked so hard he almost went lightheaded at the thought of that mouth on his cock, sucking with the same brutal intensity. He shoved her tank top up to her armpits and took a second to appreciate the sight of her pale cleavage swelling above a red, push-up bra. "Sex hiatus?"

"Yeah." She was on the move again, raining hot little kisses along the side of his neck. "Fun's fun, but I figured it was time to stop making the same mistakes with the same old guys."

He reached behind her and unclasped her bra. Her breasts sprang free from their satin and lace restraint. Compact, upswept, with tight, pink nipples pointed straight at him. His mouth watered with anticipation. "Time to make a new mistake, with a new guy?"

She laughed, and the low husky sound pulled his attention back to her face. Her grin slipped a bit off center as she stared at him and smoothed her hand along his cheek. "This is, without a doubt, a huge mistake."

He didn't know if she was trying to warn herself off, or him, but it didn't matter. Good judgment had abandoned him the second he'd walked into her shop, or, in truth, the minute he'd left the house this evening, knowing full well where he'd end up. "Then we better make it count. One night. No apologies. No regrets."

A wiggle of her hips served as a cue to put her down. For a moment of staggering disappointment he thought she'd changed her mind, but when he put her on her feet, she leaned over and dug around in the bottom drawer of her workstation. A second later she straightened and tossed a handful of condoms onto the surface. She stared at him in the mirror and added, "I'm a big believer in no regrets."

To show her she wouldn't have any, he hitched up her skirt, yanked her tiny, red thong out of his way, freed his throbbing cock from his jeans and nestled it along the cleft of her ass.

Her mouth dropped open and her eyes went wide. "Holy mother...load."

"You don't know the half of it...well...maybe about half." And he was only half-joking, which must have shown on his face because she wrapped her hands around the edge of the counter in front of her and shivered.

"Are you going to sweet talk me, or dirty talk me, before you—?"

"I'm going to fuck you." So saying, he reached past her, grabbed a condom and tore it open.

"Oh, God, okay, that works." He got the condom on, then reached around and sent his fingers into the neatly groomed, gratifyingly damp strip of red curls between her thighs.

"Until you scream my name, sweet Virginia," he added, just to see what she'd toss back, and gave her a slow, thorough stroke.

"Sugar…" She leaned into the workstation and raised her hips to give him more access. "I don't even remember your name."

How had he resisted her for two weeks? He laughed, but the laugh was on him, because he was the one who wouldn't survive their night of no regrets. Her heat, the feel of her, slick on his fingers as she grinded against his hand, and the slow, condom-lubricated slide of his cock along the ripe-peach contours of her backside had his mind racing with a thousand possibilities, and his body ached to act on them all at once. Incompatible impulses he scrambled to organize and prioritize. Kiss her until their lips went raw. Take her breast into his mouth and suck her nipple so she felt the pull all the way down her spine. Drop to his knees and devour her until she came with a scream and coated his tongue with her taste. But all of that was impossible, because the strongest urge, the one forcing its way to the forefront, involved one thing only—him sliding into her slick, tight heat, and losing himself there, fucking her so long, so hard, they'd both have scars by the time he was done.

Seven months suddenly struck him as a reckless amount of time to have gone without an orgasm involving another living, breathing, *feeling* human being, with needs and priorities of her own. He was like a ticking time bomb.

She arched her back and came up on her toes, squeezing his cock again in the process.

Jesus. He slid one finger inside her. She sucked in a breath and went higher on her toes. He eased another finger in. Her body clenched around him and she let out a small, impatient "Now."

"Take another finger," he whispered.

"No more. I want you."

He worked the third finger in anyway, because what came next was a hell of a lot more than three fingers. "I want to make sure you're ready. Otherwise, when this is all over, you'll be cursing me for the next week."

"I've been cursing you for the last two. What's one more?"

There it went. The end of his rope. He pushed her down until her forearms rested on the surface of her workstation. "Hold on, sweet Virginia, we're about to find out." With that, he drove into her. In some detached, disassociated part of his mind, he heard her cry out…first a high-pitched gasp, which slowly tumbled into a long, soul-deep groan.

Experience told him to stay still and let her adjust. Keep his hand cupped to her body, stroke her so she moved against him, pushing back as he pushed forward, finding a pace she liked. Basically, hold himself in check until she'd worked herself into a frenzy. But tonight the voice of need overrode the voice of experience, and demanded more. More. Deeper.

Harder. Faster. He pumped his hips in an insatiable, instinctive urge to find what his body craved. Blood rushed in his ears. His heartbeat thundered in his chest. Tremors started somewhere around his calves and worked their way up.

Virginia clamped around him like a fist, over, and over, and over again, and called his name. And still it wasn't enough. Not for him.

"I need more of you…all of you," he ground out.

She raised her head, looked in the mirror, and her frantic gaze crashed into him "Please, please, please Shaun…I have to come now. I don't care what you do, or how you do it. Just…fucking…do it."

Chapter Four

From somewhere over the runaway train of blood pumping in her ears, Ginny heard herself calling Shaun's name. More than once, and fairly desperately. *Pride goeth before the fall.* But hell's bells, she hadn't been prepared for this fall.

Okay, yes, she'd had sex—maybe more than her fair share—for the fun of it, or to relieve the boredom of another predictable Bluelick Friday night, or for the ego-validation of the conquest. Sometimes playful, sometimes sweet, sometimes purely physical, but never anything like this. Shaun's urgency made her feel as necessary as a heartbeat, as important as oxygen, and the ruthless honesty of his need wrung a response from her she hadn't dreamed existed. She might as well have been the virgin he'd teased about, because now, in this moment, she found herself grappling with symptoms she didn't understand, and had no idea how to deal with, and she would have offered him anything, opened up to him in any way he demanded, as long as he delivered the relief his touch promised.

I need more of you. All of you, he'd said.

She couldn't fathom what more she had to offer, given he had her bent over a workstation and filled to the bursting point while she danced on the edge of the most crucial orgasm of her entire life, but she'd take it. All of it.

Long, blunt-tipped fingers glided over her jaw. Then he cupped her chin, traced her lips, and slid two fingers inside. A shockingly intimate and inexplicably controlling move—as if he intended to invade and possess every part of her. Even though the notion disturbed her, she couldn't help tightening her lips to keep him there.

He groaned his approval, then took a deep breath, opened his eyes and met hers in the mirror. "It's about to get rough."

Her inner walls spasmed at the prospect. And then he was moving again. Every powerful thrust rocked her forward, forcing the breath out of her lungs, shoving her swollen, aching parts into his waiting palm down below, pushing the fingers of his other hand deeper into her mouth. Every withdrawal pulled her back, gave her a fleeting moment to inhale and try to rub against his hand in her own personal rhythm before he slammed into her again and bounced her around like a small aircraft caught in turbulence.

He surrounded her, filled her so he was all she could taste, all she could breathe. She sweated him out her pores. The ache inside tightened, and twisted, and turned so sharp she couldn't focus on anything else. Her muscles quivered against the ferocity of what was coming. She heard him grunt, and in some remote part of her mind she knew she was biting his fingers and ought to relax her jaw, but then he thrust again and relaxing any part of her body became impossible. She whimpered and trembled as the world started to crumble and fall away.

Another thrust. A low, groaning curse, and then a shudder shook his rugged frame. She clung to the workstation and raised her head to watch him. Their eyes met just before his went dark and glazed. He whispered, "Come for me, sweet Virginia."

She did, with a soul-crushing force, and his name on her lips.

• • •

"Something is definitely wrong when I'm the pace-setter." Melody's teasing jibe didn't hide the hint of concern in her voice. Ginny inwardly grimaced and picked up her speed as they jogged along the magnolia-flanked perimeter of the freshly mowed town square.

"Maybe I'm going easy on you because of your… ahem…condition?"

"Oh, please. A thirty-minute, three-mile jog at lunchtime is perfectly fine for a healthy woman in her first trimester. Besides," Melody wiped the glow from her forehead and Ginny caught the glint of her friend's brand new engagement ring. "Ellie cleared it."

"Good to know."

"Right, but you're still going slower than normal." Mel's long, blonde ponytail swished as she turned and looked at Ginny. "Are you second-guessing my boss?"

"Who, me? Hell no. I'm just a hairdresser. I'm not going to second-guess Dr. Ellie Swann."

"Okay then, since we've established there's no need to go slow for me, it must be for you. Why so pokey today?"

Ginny glanced around to see if anyone stood within earshot, but the coast was clear. "Um, because I got poked last night. Repeatedly."

Melody skidded to a stop. "What?"

Ginny kept running, but slowed to give her friend a chance to catch up. "Now who's the pokey one?"

"Still you, apparently. Details, please. Who? When? Where? How? And most importantly, why? I thought you were on a sex hiatus."

"Geez, let's see. Wolverine. Last night. At the salon, after I closed. Given your condition, I think you know how. I'm a little fuzzy on the *why* part myself other than he's so damn hot, because I'm not sure I even like the cocky so-and-so. And yes, I think it's safe to say the sex hiatus ended with a bang. Technically, a series of bangs. More like a fireworks finale."

"Wow." Melody's sky-blue eyes went wide as she absorbed the information. "This is so… I don't even know where to start. No, wait," she quickly corrected, "I do. Start with the fireworks finale. Tell me everything. Evvvvrything."

Ginny didn't bother holding back a grin. "Those pregnancy hormones are really raging, aren't they?"

Melody rolled her eyes. "Constantly. You have no idea. Poor Josh practically has to hose me down just to get a food break."

"Good thing he's the fire chief. I imagine he's very proficient with his…hose."

"Amen. Hallelujah. Sadly, he's on duty tonight. The only fireworks I can expect for the next twenty-four hours have to come from you. Get to it. What went down, or should I say who?"

"For such an innocent face, you have a very dirty mind. I'm not giving you the blow-by-blow—no pun intended—all I can say is, it was spontaneous and unbelievably hot and—"

"And more than once, right? I believe you promised me multiples."

"At my workstation, on the reception desk. I'm not even sure what happened under the bonnet dryer. I think I might have lost consciousness around my fourth or fifth orgasm."

Melody tapered her strides. "Sweet mercy. No wonder you're running slow today. I'm surprised you can walk."

"'Hurts so good' as the song says."

"Did you invite him back sometime soon to hurt you some more?"

"No." She shook her head and fended off the flare of regret her hormones shot toward her brain—the same brain that had abandoned her last night, as soon as Shaun had looked at her with those haunted brown eyes and touched her cheek with unexpected gentleness for such a rough, tough, badass of a guy.

"No? Why no?"

"Last night was a spontaneous, one-time-only type thing. We both agreed." Right. So why did she sound as if she was trying to convince herself? And worse, why was there a part of her that refused to be convinced? "I have other stuff to focus on. I filed my paperwork and petitions to run for mayor this morning."

"For real?"

She nodded, feeling a little glow that had nothing to do with working up a sweat in the midday sunshine.

"I'm so proud of you. This town would be lucky to have you as mayor. You care about the community. You have great, workable ideas on how to improve things." Her friend paused a moment to breathe, and then went on, "So wait. Was running for mayor what inspired your now-doomed sex hiatus?"

"Yes, but it's not doomed. Admittedly, I got swept away by brooding eyes and a tight ass, and I took one short detour off the straight and narrow, but I'm back on my path." *Yes, you are, Ginny Boca*, she silently added when some stupid part of her started to weaken. If she had to avoid the man from here on out to ensure she kept her hands off him, so be it. *Or maybe he'll avoid you?* The depressing thought fluttered through her mind like a moth. He seemed to have mastered the art of keeping a low profile.

"There's a man wandering around town who can give you four or five orgasms in one night and you're sticking to the sex hiatus? You're a strong woman."

If only. "I want to win this election, which means I need to keep my reputation clean. Cleaner than Tom Buchanan's at any rate," she added when Melody shot her an *are you smoking crack* look, "because our esteemed incumbent is the only other candidate. Behaving better than Tom shouldn't be difficult, considering he could take lessons in fidelity from a stray dog, but the last thing I should do this point in my life is take on a fuck-buddy. Nothing, I mean nothing, stays secret around here long. Why hand Tom the grounds to accuse me of having my head in my pants instead of on the problems and issues of Bluelick?"

"Yeah." Melody winced at the idea, and then waved to old Ms. Van Hendler taking her afternoon stroll along the path on the opposite end of the square. "I see your point about guarding your rep. The campaign could get ugly. Tom won't go down without a fight, and the Buchanans have never been afraid to sling a little mud. It's a family tradition."

"Exactly. I haven't spoken to Tom yet, but when I do, I'm going to tell him I hope we can stick to the issues and avoid personal attacks."

"Nice strategy, but even if he agrees to your face to keep the campaign professional, you might find you're the only one taking the high road."

"I'm aware, and I don't trust him, which is why I don't intend to hand him a big, dirty mud-ball to fling my way. He'll need to dig up his own if that's how he wants to play things. But if he does, he'll learn pretty quick I've got good aim, too."

She raised her hand and ticked off her list on her fingers. "Infidelity. A nasty divorce. A hasty marriage to a cocktail waitress half his age. And Justin." She lowered her hand. "Let's not forget Justin, who is a complete menace, and will likely stay that way as long as Tom continues to misuse the powers of his office to clean up after the spoiled brat."

"You've got that right," Melody agreed. "Justin is one of the main reasons Josh wants Tom voted out. Tom and Sheriff Butler are buddies, and Tom gets Butler to intercede whenever an investigation seems likely to implicate Justin in some wrongdoing. Josh wholeheartedly supports your idea of taking the money Bluelick pays to contract with the county sheriff's department and using it to establish our own local police department. One free from the influence of Tom Buchanan."

Ginny shrugged. "The funds are there. All it takes is a

vote from the city council. If I'm elected, I guarantee we'll put it to a vote. And when I point out each and every way the services we get from the county are substandard, I know they'll approve letting the contract lapse and earmarking those funds for a local PD."

"You've got my vote," Melody said as they jogged across Main and turned to run along the sidewalk. "Though I'm sorry your political ambitions are interfering with your personal affairs, so to speak."

Me, too. "It's for the best." She pushed aside a wave of disappointment and did an automatic scan of the street…to *avoid* him. "Besides, I didn't get the sense Shaun was looking for a repeat."

"Wolverine's real name is Shaun?"

"Yep."

"What's his last name?"

"We didn't get to last names."

Ginny kept her eyes trained on the sidewalk in front of them, but she felt Melody's sharp, blue gaze cut her way. "You got to five orgasms but no last name? Girl, you're slipping. I used to be able to rely on you for all the local intel. I expected you to know exactly who he is, where he's from, what he's doing here, and at least a couple of his deepest, darkest secrets."

"Look, it's not like I didn't ask, but he kept his cards very close to his vest, and then he distracted me with his giant dick, and—"

"And a bunch of orgasms—"

"Right. When I woke up at dawn, naked in my shampoo chair with a cape for a blanket"—*and a note that read, "Thanks for the haircut, sweet Virginia"*—"he wasn't around to answer my questions." Except one she shouldn't have been harboring in the first place, namely, *Want to do this again?* He'd answered that question loud and clear with his stealthy exit and pithy little note.

"Wait." Melody skidded to a stop. "He left you alone, naked, and asleep in your salon? What an inconsiderate imbecile. Anybody could have walked in."

"This concerned me at first, too, but it turns out he left me alone, naked, and asleep in my *locked* salon."

Melody scrunched her brow. "He took your keys?"

"Nope. My keys were in my purse, where I'd left them."

"But...your door locks from the outside. How'd he do that?"

She'd asked herself the very same question. "I don't know," she admitted, then moved closer to Melody to avoid a cluster of people coming out of DeShay's Diner. "Wolverine's got skills."

Chapter Five

The noise and constant movement of people inside the busy diner set Shaun's nerves on edge, undoing the endorphin rush of last night's haircut, as well as the positive effects of a rare eight solid hours of dreamless, uninterrupted sleep. Seeking the illusion of escape from the crowded restaurant, he glanced out the window, and nearly did a double take when he caught a flash of red hair in his peripheral vision. Sure enough, sweet Virginia zipped by, looking sleek and sexy in her high-cut jog top and low, snug shorts. A taller blonde woman jogged with her, but he had a hard time registering much else because they passed, and then, inevitably, his eyes fastened on those slim, almost coltish legs, and her truly spectacular ass. All the din of DeShay's receded to a peaceful hum. He watched until she disappeared from view.

Mr. Sentimental south of his belt buckle immediately sat up and begged for a reunion. Luckily, the table hid the reaction from any onlookers, including the man sitting opposite him in the booth.

He shifted his attention back to his father, who was talking away, oblivious to the fact his audience had tuned out. Aside from Shaun's future, which Shaun didn't particularly want to discuss, they had few shared interests and even fewer shared experiences. Conversation didn't flow naturally and easily between them. Tom was trying though, possibly out of concern for his eldest son's isolationist tendencies, if the invitation to join him at the busiest lunch spot in town served as any indication. The least he could do was pay attention.

"…when I asked for the divorce, I expected Monica to take it hard, you know, emotionally, but I never dreamed she'd turn into such a calculating bitch."

Oh yeah, that's why he'd tuned out. His dad was surprisingly clueless about the women he got involved with. "Monica *never* struck you as calculating? Maybe around the time she started seeing you—a married man? Or when she gave you the home-wrecker ultimatum?"

His dad shrugged. "I couldn't see past her face. And that body." He smiled at whatever picture his mind called up. "You're too young to remember, but Monica, twenty years ago, was a sight to behold. I'm telling you, the things she would do to me, and let me do to her—"

"Hey, look. There's the line."

His father's forehead wrinkled. "What line?"

"The one we shouldn't cross, as father and son."

Now Tom laughed. "C'mon. We're adults here. Didn't your grandfather and I take you to your first titty bar down in Annapolis when you turned twenty-one?"

"That was different." Also much closer to his last titty bar than his first, but he didn't feel the need to share every damn thing. "Sitting in a titty bar didn't force me to think about you having sex with my stepmother." Mercifully, he wasn't thinking of them at all, but rather sweet Virginia, laid out across her reception counter, arm flung over her eyes, heels digging into his chest, praying to God, and Jesus and, if his ears hadn't deceived him, Wolverine, in each short silence between the sounds of their bodies slapping together.

"Pfft. Stepmother." Tom waved the word away, and Shaun's highly entertaining flashback disappeared as well. "Some mother she turned out to be, step or otherwise. Since the divorce, she's been living it up in Atlanta on the king's ransom of alimony she demanded, sucking me dry and completely ignoring our son."

"Justin's almost eighteen. From what I can tell, he's not pining for Mommy."

"No, maybe not." Tom ran his hand over his still thick, dark hair. "But would it kill her to take him down to Atlanta for the summer? Brandi and Justin do *not* get along. I feel like a damn referee in my own home. Plus Brandi keeps harping on about us having some 'alone time'. Say…maybe you and Justin could—"

"No."

"Just for a weekend. He can help you fix up the cabin. Give you two a chance to bond like brothers."

"No."

"It would be good for both of you."

"Only if you consider double homicide good. Send him to attitude adjustment camp, or…fuck…I don't know…prep school."

"Even if I could interest him in going, it's financially impossible. The wedding and honeymoon set me back. Then

Brandi got it in her head she needed to redecorate the house, because it 'reeked of Monica'. Meanwhile, Monica's alimony is cleaning me out. Everything is compounded by the fact that some of my investments took a bad dip recently. Times are tight. Justin will get access to his trust fund when he turns eighteen, thank God, so I don't have to fret about how to pay for his college, but the trustee won't allow me to crack into it early just to send him somewhere for the summer."

Tom paused for breath, smoothed his hair again, and then glanced around the diner. "And now I'm going to have to spend money I don't have on a mayoral campaign, because some bimbo decided to run against me."

"Sorry to hear about your financial problems." And he was, even if those problems stemmed mostly from his father's expensive personal choices. Despite the current bind, Tom had offered him the family-owned cabin at the outskirts of town for as long as he wanted, and steadfastly refused any discussion of rent. Shaun's mother often referred to his father as "the most emotionally selfish, yet ridiculously generous man I ever knew." Mom had re-married a couple years after the divorce—to a nice, stable guy who adored everything about her—and hadn't wasted her breath bashing her ex. She simply spoke the truth. Tom equated money with affection, and he'd slowly but surely populated his life with people willing to exploit that tendency—Monica, Brandi, Justin, and the list no doubt went on.

"Let me pay rent for the cabin."

"No." His father shook his head. "Family doesn't charge rent, especially not when you're putting sweat equity into the place, updating it and whatnot. You need a place to stay while you"—he made a vague gesture—"figure out your next step. The cabin's available. Done deal."

"All right. Why don't I float you a loan? I didn't use my trust fund for school, so—"

"No, no. You need your funds. Now that you're done with the SEALs, you may decide to get a graduate degree, or start a business…or volunteer as my campaign manager."

He had no plans to do any of the above, but saying so would turn the conversation to just what the hell he did plan to do, now that plan A—working for the county sheriffs— had fallen through. Since he didn't have a fucking clue, he stayed clear of that particular minefield. "Look, I can't baby-sit Justin for you. That would never work. But leaving him to kick around Bluelick all summer is a disaster waiting to happen. You'll end up cracking open his trust fund to make bail, or worse. I can lend you the money to park Justin somewhere productive and character-building for the next little while."

"Justin's going through a tough time, at a tough age. We'll get through it." Tom's glance slid away, out the window. "I've a couple eggs tucked away in a basket. If everything goes as planned, I expect them to hatch shortly after the election."

That should have made him feel better, but the crowd and the noise in the diner suddenly seemed oppressive. A weight of apprehension settled in his gut. *Time to go*. He stood and tossed some bills on the table. "Good to hear, but let me know if you change your mind. One thing I learned in the SEALs is that plans go sideways, and eggs have a tendency to break— especially when you tuck them away in one basket."

Tom blinked at him for a second, and then the corner of his mouth tipped up and he shook his head. "Were you always this smart?"

Shaun picked up the Wildcats ball cap he'd stowed in

the booth and put it on his head. "When it comes to learning lessons the hard way, I'm a fucking genius."

• • •

You're a fucking idiot. This wasn't the first time tonight the voice in Shaun's head had chimed in with the helpful opinion, but it hadn't stopped him from ending up here, walking the dark, empty sidewalks of downtown Bluelick.

A glance at his watch told him it was just shy of nine. Small towns, however, rolled up early, even on a Friday night. There might be a few late diners at DeShay's, and Rawley's was probably packed, but he'd been down this road enough to know unless Virginia had a late customer, she closed at six on Fridays. From across the street he looked at the dimly lit storefronts.

Turn around and go home. She won't be there.

Then there's no harm in walking past.

You're a fucking idiot.

Maybe. Okay, yes, he was, because his pulse kicked up when he saw the salon door swing open. She stepped out, and the light from inside put sparks of amber in her hair. She wore one of those flimsy sundresses with thin shoulder straps and a short, ruffly skirt. A woven leather belt emphasized her tiny waist and black cowboy boots emphasized her slender legs. She hefted her big, black purse onto her shoulder and then turned to lock up.

A dark figure rocketed down the sidewalk, sideswiped her hard enough to send her to the ground, and kept moving.

"Hey!" Shaun leapt off the curb and gave chase, picking up speed as he cut diagonally across the street and closed in on the retreating figure. The guy had something in his hand. Not a gun. Not a knife. Not anything big or heavy, apparently, because the skinny little fucker moved like the wind. He had a lead, and he could haul ass well enough to hold onto it. Meanwhile, Virginia was somewhere behind him, possibly injured. Shaun slowed, turned around at the corner and ran back to the salon.

She was cursing and picking the contents of her purse off the sidewalk, but she looked up when he approached. "Get him?"

He shook his head. "Nope. Couldn't even swear it was a him. Are you okay?"

"I'm fine. Pissed, but fine." She accepted his hand and let him pull her to her feet.

Light from inside the salon poured through the open door. The yellow sundress was actually a lemon print, she wore dangly earrings with a cascade of green stones the exact shade as her eyes, and she had a small scratch on the underside of her chin where it had connected with the sidewalk. Temper burned through him at the sight—a temper he recognized as completely out of proportion to the situation, but was unable to get a leash on. "What the hell were you doing, leaving work all alone, at this time of night?"

She gave him an exasperated look. "Are you serious?"

Before he could answer, she shook her head, sending the earrings dancing, and slapped her hand against the center of his chest. "No, you know what? You're right. What was I thinking, staying late at my place of business to finish up a bunch of paperwork, and then braving the mean streets of Bluelick on my own? Having lived here…oh…all my *life*, I should know better. Back in 1997 some criminal mastermind broke into Dalton's and stole a six-pack of beer. Shit gets serious around here after dark."

He knew he owed her an apology, for jumping on her—the victim—because the asshole who deserved his temper had outrun him, but what came out of his mouth instead was, "It could have gotten serious tonight, if I hadn't been here."

She rolled her eyes, which lit another charge under his already volatile temper, but then she gingerly touched her fingers to the sore spot on her chin, and the small gesture immediately defused his anger.

"What *are* you doing here?"

"I was walking."

Those keen green eyes found their way back to him. "Walking?" She looked around at the closed businesses along the street. "Walking where?"

Heat crawled up his neck. *Busted.* "Nowhere. I was just walking, and... Look, it doesn't matter. What matters is somebody was out here tonight, and he jumped you, and it might not have ended there—"

"He didn't jump me." She put air quotes around the phrase. "He bumped into me. I surprised him when I came out the door. He ran, knocked me over, and kept on running. What I'd really like to know is what the hell he was doing hanging around outside my salon."

With the question hanging in the air, they both looked in the direction he'd come. There, on the whitewashed brick exterior wall, someone had written the word "firecrotch" in red spray-paint.

She marched over, touched the paint with a fingertip, and then kicked the wall with the toe of her boot. "Lovely. Just what I needed." Shoulders sagging, palm to her forehead, she stood there looking so uncharacteristically small and forlorn, he actually fought a rogue impulse to wrap his arms around her and…comfort her. As if he could comfort anybody.

He could do something, though. "Come on." He took her arm and tugged her through the door of the salon, and over to one of the two guest chairs set up in the waiting area—one of the few pieces of furniture in the entire place that didn't hold some memory of him buried deep inside her, letting her body exorcise every ragged frustration, every gnawing anxiety eating at him, hungrily absorbing everything she had to give. And if he kept thinking about last night, he'd never… "Sit."

"You are all kinds of bossy," she snapped, but she sat. That's when he noticed she'd skinned her knee, too, and had a red patch on her arm.

"First aid kit?"

"It's in the cabinet under the sink in the bathroom. In back. I'll get it—"

"Stay." Hands on her shoulders, he re-planted her in the chair.

"This may come as a shock to you, but I'm not a dog," she called after him.

Jesus, Buchanan, get your shit under control. He caught his reflection in the mirror above the sink and almost groaned. *Try to look a little less like you're on a suicide mission.* Kit in hand, he relaxed his jaw, took a deep breath, and then walked back into the salon. After a quick stop at the shampoo sink to wet a hand towel, he made his way to where she sat, watching him.

He snagged the other chair, positioned it in front of hers, and sat down facing her.

"Dr. Feelgood, I presume?"

"Something like that. You have a phone in your bag?" He gestured to the purse she'd placed beside her chair.

"Yes."

He opened the first aid kit. "Call the sheriff's department. Ask them to send someone out to take a report."

"Nothing will come of it. I didn't see the guy, and neither did you, so they won't do anything."

"They'll take the report. Maybe our wall artist gets caught next time he's out expressing himself, and the sheriff can charge him with vandalism and battery for tonight, too."

She eyed him skeptically, but dug her phone out of her bag, did a search, and dialed. "You give the county sheriffs more credit than they deserve—Hello? Yes, I'd like to report a crime."

He cleaned her knee as carefully as possible while she spoke to the sheriff's department. The scrape was superficial, but he dabbed antibacterial cream on and covered it with a Band-Aid.

She ended the call and dropped her phone back into her bag, then looked at her leg. "I don't think I've worn a Band-Aid on my knee since I was seven." As she spoke she absently fiddled with the front of his hair. She probably didn't even realize it, but he registered her touch immediately, and knew he'd nursed his way back into her good graces.

"It will help keep the cut clean until a scab forms. You can take it off in a little while."

"Speaking of a little while, county dispatch said there's a car in the area. A deputy should be here in a few minutes." Her hand fell away from his hair, rested on his shoulder for a moment, and then withdrew altogether. "I can take it from here. Don't feel like you have to stick around."

"I'm a witness." He used the towel to clean the raw spot on her arm. She sucked in a breath and he immediately lightened his touch. "Sorry." His thumb caressed the skin on the inside of her arm, and inadvertently brushed the outer swell of her breast. The room shrank and got about a thousand degrees hotter.

Her eyes darted to his and then, just as quickly, bounced away, and even though he couldn't read minds, he knew she was thinking about last night. "I'm okay."

What part of last night was she thinking of? "You are way better than okay." He put antibacterial cream on the wound and covered it with another Band-Aid, then tipped her head up and turned his attention to the scrape on her chin.

"Was that a line, Shaun? You're going to make me think you weren't serious about last night being a mistake."

Don't. "Were you?" He leaned in closer…to tend to the scrape, and inhaled her lemon and honey scent.

"I was, at the time, yes. I have really good reasons for wanting to avoid any, um, mistakes right now. But…"

Don't do it. "But"—he waited until she lowered her chin and looked at him—"some mistakes are worth repeating?"

A pulse hammered at the base of her throat. "If we could keep things on the down lo—"

"County Sheriff!" A knock rattled the door at the same time the deputy announced himself. Ginny jumped about a mile.

"Good God." She closed her eyes and rested her palm on her heart, as if to calm it, then opened them and smiled up at him in a way that made him want to calm *his* heart. "Who said there's never a cop around when you need one?"

Chapter Six

Ginny's stomach sank a bit when she saw the tall, lanky, crew-cut blond with ice-chip blue eyes staring back at her through the door of the salon. Another deputy—a forty-something bald guy with a beer gut overhanging his utility belt—stood there as well, but thankfully she didn't recognize him. She unlocked and held the door open for them. "Hey, Trent." She gave him a quick hug.

"Hey Ginny." Trent Sullivan returned the hug and then pulled back and flashed the orthodontist-perfected smile that had made him the most popular lifeguard at the Bluelick municipal pool when they'd been teenagers. He'd gotten taller and filled out some since then, but he'd changed very little in the year or so since she'd last hooked up with him on a Saturday night at Rawley's after one too many white wines.

Hoping to avoid an ill-timed trip down memory lane, she jumped on the first safe topic that sprang to mind and tapped the badge on his chest. "You joined the sheriff's department?"

Trent squared his shoulders and struck a pose. "Chicks dig the uniform." His smile deepened as he looked her over, issuing a not-so-subtle invitation. And why wouldn't he? It had worked for him in the past.

"You look very official." She glanced over at Shaun, who was doing his silent observer thing. Was he feeling jealous? Territorial?

He raised one dark eyebrow at her, and she caught the faintest trace of a grin on his unfairly irresistible lips. Completely unfazed. That's what he was. As if he knew damn well he'd wrung responses out of her body last night that nobody else had come close to achieving...including her. The arrogant so-and-so. If he dared call her sweet Virginia right now, she'd strangle him with her bare hands.

Jebus, you've had sex with two-thirds of the men in this room. Was this fate's way of reminding her why she'd instituted the sex hiatus in the first place? If so, it might be too little, too late, because the cocky thing totally worked on her...no white wine needed. It worked so well, she took a minute to realize Trent was still talking.

"...so then I got on board with the sheriff's department earlier this year, completed my eighteen weeks at the Department of Criminal Justice in Rochester a few months ago. I've been riding shotgun with Deputy Crocker here since then."

Ginny stuck out her hand. "Deputy Crocker."

"Virginia Boca," Trent provided, while the older man chewed on a toothpick and shook her hand.

"Miz Boca."

"And this," she turned to Shaun, and realized she was

about to learn his last name, "is my…um…my friend—"

"Hey Shaun," Trent said and stepped forward. "Long time no see." The two men shook hands.

Deputy Crocker lifted his chin in greeting. "Shaun."

"Crocker."

So much for learning his last name. She didn't know whether to be intrigued or worried by the fact he seemed to be on a first-name basis with the deputies, but she didn't have a chance to give the issue much thought because Crocker sent Trent outside to take pictures of the graffiti and canvass the area for any additional evidence. Then the older deputy produced a clipboard and a form, and starting peppering her with questions. He took her statement, interrupting several times to "clarify" facts she'd been perfectly clear about. She didn't consider herself an especially short-tempered person, but getting run over by some asshole after he painted a rude name on her wall and putting up with the skeptical third-degree from Crocker worked her last nerve.

Then he took Shaun's statement, and her hackles rose even more. Crocker accepted Shaun's version of events—which corresponded perfectly with hers—without hesitation or a single second-guess. As if a penis automatically made him a reliable witness, while her lack of one made her some kind of hysterical drama queen. If Shaun hadn't been there, Crocker wouldn't have listened to a word she said.

Or maybe good ole boy sexism didn't explain why Crocker treated her like a second class citizen? Maybe the news of her running for mayor had reached the sheriff's department? If so, Crocker's attitude offered a strong indication they endorsed her opponent. Big surprise.

"Okay, Miz Boca." Crocker turned back to her. "Let's

run through this again. Can you describe the person who spray-painted your wall and pushed you down?"

"Deputy, I've already told you I didn't see him. I was locking up, and then I was doing my impersonation of a tackle dummy, and then I was on the sidewalk, seeing stars."

The man gave a long-suffering sigh. "Short? Tall?"

"I don't know. Shaun said—"

"I heard what he said. I'm asking you."

She closed her eyes to block out the red hazing her vision and slowly counted to ten. "I didn't see."

"Dark coloring? Light? Any tattoos or distinguishing marks?"

"I. Don't. Know."

"Crocker," Shaun started, and the realization he felt the need to take control of the situation stretched the ragged leash she had on her temper. She hadn't wanted to call the sheriff in the first place, but she sure as hell didn't need Shaun rescuing her from this jerk.

"Let's just take the gloves off, okay? I know who it was. You know who it was. We both know you're not going to do a damn thing about it."

Trent slammed back into the salon, and stopped short at the tension in the room. He looked questioningly between her and Crocker.

"Miz Boca," Crocker replied, "I can assure you, based on the statements provided to us tonight we have no suspects at this time. Now, if you have additional information you'd like to add to your statement—"

"Justin Buchanan." She spat the name at him. From the corner of her eye, she saw Shaun's head swivel her way, but she was too intent on watching Crocker's reaction to abide by any cautions Shaun might have been attempting to convey.

"You think it was Justin Buchanan?"

"I know it was. I just can't prove it. Put that in your report."

Crocker looked at Shaun. "Was it Justin?"

As if Shaun's word was gospel and hers, garbage.

"I told you—"

"I can't say," Shaun cut her off. "I didn't get a clear look. Size-wise, he's a possibility, but going strictly by size, a lot of people fit the description."

Crocker gave her a "there you go" look.

And Shaun's answer *was* the reasonable one. Deep down, she knew it. Too bad she'd lost her grip on reasonable around the time Crocker had shown up and treated her like the girl who cried wolf. "I've lived here my whole life, Deputy. Shaun's been in town a matter of months. I'd love to know why in God's name you'd place more weight on his opinion than mine."

"Because I think Shaun here might recognize his own brother."

"His own…" *What?* Crocker's sentence sank in. A cold sensation spread from her chest to her stomach. She turned and stared at Shaun.

"Your brother?" Though it came out as a question, she already knew the answer. She could see the Buchanan on him clear as day now—hair, eyes, jawline. He'd been a grade ahead of her in elementary school. A tall, long-limbed preteen who'd transferred schools after his dad had remarried.

He looked back at her, his patented mask of stoicism in place. "Half brother."

"You're Shaun-freaking-Buchanan? I can't believe you

held back your last name. Didn't you think that minor detail would be material to me?" Then a darker, meaner thought slithered into her mind. She hissed out a breath and narrowed her eyes. "Or were you playing me the whole time you were"—remembering they had an audience, she fumbled for some not-too-compromising way to reference last night—"in my chair?"

"I'm not *playing* anyone. I didn't tell you my last name because I'd just as soon keep a low profile while I'm here, and avoid the small town soap opera. I didn't consider it material to anyone but me."

Yeah, right. She folded her arms across her chest and told herself to drop it. Now wasn't the time to dig into the matter, because she didn't need the deputies suspecting she'd done the deed with her opponent's son. Neither Trent nor Crocker would keep a tidbit like that to themselves, and once the rumor started circulating her mayoral campaign would be over. But even so, she couldn't stop herself from saying, "I don't believe you."

"Virginia, I haven't spent time in Bluelick since I was twelve. I have no fucking clue who's feuding with whom, or who's got an ax to grind with my family. All I know about the local situation is"—he broke off and visibly racked his brain for an example—"some bimbo is running for mayor."

Trent had the good grace to feign a cough, but Crocker burst out laughing.

She glared at Shaun. "*I'm* the bimbo."

• • •

Told you you're a fucking idiot. Shaun pressed the gas pedal to the floor and steered the Wrangler up Riverview Road, but no matter how hard he pushed the engine, he couldn't outrun the voice in his head. The woman he'd developed an unwilling fascination for, the one with whom he'd spent the most consuming, mind-blowing night in God-only-knew-how-long, wanted to oust his father from office, send his half-brother to juvie, and, about now, tear *his* balls off.

Irony lifted the corners of his mouth into a tight smile. Last night she'd warned him they were making a mistake, but neither of them had appreciated what an understatement the prediction would turn out to be.

Not much he could do about that particular situation, but he could try to address tonight's first unpleasant surprise. Unlike the deputies, he didn't need probable cause to question Justin about his whereabouts this evening. He turned into the circular driveway and parked by the front door, frowning as he noted the house lit up like a stadium, but no other cars in the drive.

The home boasted a three-car garage, so the lack of a red mustang in the driveway didn't mean Justin wasn't around. Ingrained training had him leveraging the element of surprise. He twisted the front door handle. It gave. He walked into the empty entryway in time to see Brandi pause on the way down the big, central staircase and press a hand to her gravity-defying chest. A chest nearly on full display thanks to the thin, white robe she wore.

"Jesus, you scared the shit out of me."

Yeah, he got that a lot. Years spent moving quietly made the habit hard to break. "Sorry. Is Justin home?"

She shook her head, sending her white-blonde hair behind her shoulders, and continued down the stairs. "No."

"Do you happen to know where he is?"

"Don't know. Don't care." Her light brown eyes turned calculating and she smiled as she closed in on him.

Nice. "How about my father?" He held his ground, but deliberately stressed the word father.

She shook her head again. "Nope. He's in some cow-seal thingie tonight. Won't be home for another hour at least." She dragged her finger down the center of his chest.

He backed up and swallowed the bitter lump of disgust rising in his throat. "A cow-seal thingie?"

She shrugged a shoulder, utterly careless of the effect the move had on the front of her robe. "That's what he said."

"That doesn't make any... Wait a minute...a *council* meeting?"

"Um..." Her brows knitted. "Yeah. Maybe that's what he said." Her expression cleared and she sidled nearer. "Anyway, I'm bored and"—she threw a pout his way—"lonely. Come watch TV with me. There's a big, comfy sofa downstairs."

Not in this lifetime. He backed toward the door. "Sorry, Brandi. I've got stuff to take care of. You'll have to entertain yourself. Tell Tom I need to talk to him."

After "cow-seal thingie" he doubted her ability to relay the simplest message. He got into the Jeep and made a mental note to call his father tomorrow.

No wonder you're a fucking idiot. It's in your blood. Of course, with wife number three Tom had plainly sunk to a new low on the fucking idiot scale. He thought of Brandi and shook his head. To hell with blood. He was breaking the cycle, and swore a silent oath never to let his dick take charge of his life the way Tom always had. But as he drove past the closed salon, a certain pissed-off redhead filled his mind, and his dick refused to honor the oath.

He drove to the cabin, dug a brush and a can of leftover white trim paint out of the storage shed, and headed back to the salon. As he layered a couple coats of white over the crude spray-paint, he tried to talk some sense into his insubordinate body parts.

Give it a rest. She doesn't want anything to do with you now that she knows who you are, and the last thing you need is to get tangled up with your family's most outspoken opponent.

The wall was an easy fix. Him? Not so much. He loaded the supplies into the back of the Jeep, loaded himself into the front, and started the engine. Sleep was a thousand miles away and a drive sounded better than sitting alone in a dark house. The doctor he'd seen before leaving the Navy had assured him time, distance, and immersion into civilian life would eventually ease the sleep problems, and recommended medication and therapy to help bridge the journey. She'd called the insomnia and nightmares part of a transition cycle. Shaun called it yet another reason to listen to his inner voice.

Six a.m. the next morning, riding on fumes, Shaun made a left turn into the driveway behind the Gas 'n Go and slammed on his brakes to avoid hitting a blur of blue and white cutting across the alley. The blur stopped in front of his bumper, turned to him, and their eyes locked.

Sweet Virginia, out for a morning run. Sweaty,

out-of-breath, wide-eyed Virginia, looking like she didn't know whether to give him a piece of her mind or pretend he didn't exist. Their final exchange last night after the deputies had left replayed in his memory.

You deliberately didn't give me your last name because you knew I wouldn't have touched you if I'd known who you were.

Sweetheart, you're fooling yourself if you really believe knowing my name would have changed any aspect of last night.

It changes everything moving forward. There will be no repeats. In fact, it would be best for both of us if we never set eyes on each other again.

The rational, risk-mitigating part of him agreed, because every time he saw her, he wanted her, on a primitive, bone-deep level. Unfortunately, this morning already proved avoiding anyone in a town the size of Bluelick was damn near impossible...even for a man trained to disappear.

Do not engage.

He kicked the e-brake, turned off the engine, and stepped out of the Jeep. She stood there like a deer in headlights.

Body on autopilot, attention glued to her—because he felt certain she'd vanish if he so much as blinked—he closed the distance between them. When he was close enough to see the black striations in her stunning green eyes, he said, "What are you thinking, cutting through an alley at dawn?"

"I was thinking, for once, I might manage to cross a street without getting run down by a Buchanan. What kind of maniac drives into an alley like a bat out of hell?"

She was trying to sound pissed, and she didn't lay a finger on him, which, for her, he'd already pieced together, definitely signified temper, but her eyes kept straying from his to wander down his body, and each time they came back she was breathing a little bit harder.

Apparently that was all the encouragement he needed. The controlled, disciplined side of him surrendered and the reckless side took control. He wrapped his fingers around her bare biceps and tugged her around the side of the gas station. The restroom door hung open. He shoved her inside, followed, and locked the door behind him. The smell of pine cleaner and liquid soap competed with the scent of her over-heated skin. When he turned around, her lips were wet and parted, her sweet little nipples straining against the form-fitting fabric of her workout top, and her eyes shooting fire.

"Shaun Buchanan, you are so close to getting your face slapped. Do you honestly expect me to—?"

Yeah, maybe he was delusional from lack of sleep, but he did. He slammed his mouth down on hers and hauled her up against him. The toes of her running shoes scored the tile floor until he got his hands under her ass and lifted her off her feet. She wrapped her legs around his waist, fisted her hands in the front of his shirt and sucked his tongue into her mouth, which sent a rush of blood straight to his already swollen cock.

He broke away long enough to make sure they were in agreement, because he might persuade by any means necessary, but he'd never force. "I'm full of expectations. I expect you to let me peel those thin, tight, and very damp shorts down your legs. I expect you to give my mouth and tongue and hands free reign until you're biting your lip to keep from begging for more. And when I give you more, I expect you to scream my name in gratitude. If you feel the need to slap my face before, during or afterwards, go right ahead."

"Oh, God. Okay." She tightened her legs around his hips and rocked against him. "One last time…"

He murmured an agreement, even as he devoured her mouth, even as a part of him acknowledged the lie. Her taste, her scent, the weight of her wrapped around him, grounded him in some way he couldn't understand or articulate, but he knew one last time wouldn't be enough.

"Hurry," she panted when they broke for air.

He almost laughed, because taking things slow wasn't an option. A condom machine hung on the wall. He braced her beside it, and kept right on feasting on her mouth while he felt around in his pocket for change, dumped the quarters in the slot, and…waited. Nothing.

She stopped kissing him, turned, and blinked at the thieving metal rectangle, and then banged on the thing with the side of her fist. Still nothing.

"Stop." He caught her hand before she could bang it again. "Don't hurt yourself. I've got a key." He let her go and backed up a step—which was about all the space he had in the small restroom. Shifting his weight to his left leg, he swung his right leg out, and landed a power angle kick to the side of the machine. The flimsy lock popped, the metal door opened and a couple condoms fell into his waiting hand. He glanced over at her.

She had her hand flattened between her breasts and stared at the mangled machine. Then her gaze shifted to him. "Is there anything you can't get into or out of?"

He considered the words an invitation, and spun her around to face the door. Her squeak of surprise only spurred him on. "You tell me," he challenged, and tugged those snug, blue running shorts down just far enough to bare the extremely memorable ass beneath. She gasped, and then squirmed as he worked his hand between her thighs. A small cry came next when he strummed his fingers through the warm, soft, very wet valley and sank his teeth into one smooth, giving glute. Her palms flattened against the door and she rocked up onto her toes. He sealed his lips to her flesh and sucked the tender skin hard enough to leave a red mark. By the time he finished, the little cries had turned into a constant soundtrack, and the movement of her hips had become precise and determined as she worked herself against his fingers.

She was already so close. He could practically smell the orgasm on her. Practically see the energy of it gathering in her bunched-up muscles. Determined to push her straight on over, he used his free hand to grasp one perfect handful of ass cheek, spreading them, and speared his tongue into the tight little crevice.

"Oh my God!" She bucked, pumped furiously against his fingers, and then shuddered when he withdrew and proceeded to tease her with lightning-quick flicks. Her breath evened. The cries grew softer, and the muscles under his lips relaxed infinitesimally. He tightened his grip, which might have telegraphed his intention because she gasped, "Have mercy. Not again…"

"Yes, sweet Virginia, again." He drove her up, up, up, until he had her dancing on the tip of his tongue, her lush clit pulsing against the pad of his finger. Then he circled one opening with his finger and the other with his tongue, and paused there, at the thresholds. She whimpered and froze. He waited a beat just to let what was about to happen sink in, to get a sense she understood he was going to storm her defenses from all sides. She pushed back ever so slightly—a small sign of impatience and need—and all the permission he required.

He stormed. She screamed, banged the door once with her fist, and came with a long, low, grateful moan.

Chapter Seven

Slamming head-first into the orgasm—and possibly the restroom door—sent Ginny into a momentary coma. No sight. No sound. Just wave after wave of sensation crashing through her with a velocity she couldn't possibly withstand.

Luckily standing wasn't an issue. Shaun lifted her and sat her down on the only available surface—the lip of the sink. Next thing she knew, the backs of her legs were flush with his body, the heels of her running shoes hitched on his shoulders, her fingers gripping the bull-nosed porcelain for stability while he tore open his fly and rolled on a condom.

The situation turned her Lycra running shorts into a tight band tethering her thighs together. She tried to use one hand to tug the shorts down, but as soon as she let go of the sink she felt as if she'd capsize. "My shorts—"

As an answer, he simply lifted her hips a notch higher, tipping her backward until her shoulders hit the wall behind her. Then he guided himself into her still quivering sex. She watched through sweat-blurred vision as he concentrated on the task, clearly enjoying the view even as he took pains to feed himself in slowly. It was she who became restless, and impatient, and desperate for more, but the position he had her in left her a passenger on this journey. Whatever she wanted, she'd have to ask for it.

"Faster," she said. "Harder," and reinforced her hold on the sink.

He stared at her, and then slowly smiled. "You know your options, sweet Virginia."

Correction. He expected her to beg for it…or…slap his face? Okay, there was a very real possibility she'd fall, but she crunched her abs, reached up and grabbed a handful of his T-shirt and cracked her palm across his cheek. His head whipped to the side and he growled, "Jesus…"

An apology sprang to her lips, but the brutality of the need he'd generated had her biting it back and going on the defensive. "You told me to—"

"I did." He raised his head and looked at her. "I want your hands on me. I want the honesty of your touch—gently, urgently, harshly, if that's what you're feeling—but if you do that again, I'm going to come where I stand."

Then he groaned and let his head fall back, and all she could do was cling to the edge of the sink while he gave her exactly what she asked for. Thrusting, withdrawing, and thrusting again in thrilling succession, using the angle of their bodies to ensure he hit all the right spots along the way. The room spun behind her closed eyelids. A heady mix of pheromones, body heat and sex stormed her senses. With frightening speed, he had her trembling at the brink again, panting and shivering and striving for relief from the pressure building inside her. Her pulse pounded, setting off a surprisingly loud echo in her ears.

She nearly jumped out of her skin when Shaun called out, "It's occupied."

Holy crap, the pounding in her ears wasn't her pulse. Somebody was knocking on the restroom door. A voice from the other side said, "Hurry up in there buddy. I gotta get back on the road."

Shaun didn't bother with a reply, but drove into her with renewed energy, dragging her agonizingly closer to the edge of control. Her body clenched around him in a fruitless effort to cling to the moment—to a semblance of sanity—but he thrust again and sent sanity hurtling out of reach. The pressure tightened, pulsed there for one heartbeat...two... she whimpered in the face of what waited for her, and a big, calloused hand gently covered her mouth to suppress the noise.

He withdrew and rocked forward again, then froze. His eyes drifted closed, and a groan rumbled from somewhere deep in his chest.

The pounding on the door came again. "What the hell, man?"

"I'm...not...done *yet*," he growled, and unleashed a series of quick, jerky thrusts. The sink rattled on its pedestal. Between her legs, the clenching became spasms. Shaun cursed, and then groaned again, a low, long sound vibrating with relief. Hard as she tried to hold it back, her own jagged moan escaped, merging with his, outlasting it, until the high-pitched cry reverberated in the tiny room and slowly subsided.

The voice came again from the other side of the door.

"Forget it. I don't know whether you ought to burn a candle when you're done, or set fire to the place, but I know I'm not going in. See a doctor, or something."

Brown eyes opened and stared into hers, and she detected a gleam of humor in their depths. She returned his stare while footsteps retreated across pavement. After a moment, a vehicle door slammed and a big engine rumbled to life. Picturing some disgusted trucker opting for a nice, private outcropping of limestone along the Double A over what he imagined awaited him at the Gas 'n Go had her laughing on her inhale. The result was an inelegant snort.

He grinned down at her. "Admit it, I provide a refreshing break from rose petals and satin sheets."

Now she burst out laughing. A full-on, from-the-stomach laugh she couldn't have held back if her life depended on it, because damn, they'd just done it in a gas station restroom like a couple of horny teenagers. It took her a moment to stop laughing, but when she did, she smiled up at him and said, "Sugar, I'm not, and never have been, the rose petals and satin sheet type."

His expression sobered. "You are." He slipped his hand between their still-joined bodies and cupped her, massaging her gently as he slowly withdrew. Her eyes nearly rolled back in her head. "You were born for candlelight dinners and dancing barefoot under the stars." He slid out of her and she could have moaned from the loss, but his fingers were there, easing the emptiness, replacing it with warmth, while his thumb brushed the over-stimulated knot of nerves clamoring for yet more attention. "You deserve all those things, and I wish I was the man who could give them to you, but we both know I'm not. All I can give you is this—"

And he gave. And she took, knowing full well this was his way of asking if it could be enough, for as long as it lasted. Every bit of common sense in her head warned against getting into something so risky. *This has absolutely, positively got to be the last time.*

But as warmth turned to heat and the heat rolled through her, her heart sighed, *maybe.*

• • •

"Why are you so fidgety?"

LouAnn Doubletree's question pulled Ginny's head out of the clouds. "I'm not," she said to her booth-mate, and then, dang it, fidgeted.

"Oh, no. You're not fidgety, and my nickname's not Double D." LouAnn squeezed her arms together, plumping the nickname-inspiring double D's to eye-popping proportions above the scoop neck of her purple pullover. Across the diner, a busboy dropped a tray loaded with dishes. Ginny gave LouAnn a *hope you're happy* look—which the statuesque ash-blonde plainly was—and then focused on the two women in the booth opposite her.

Ellie nodded her agreement, and pushed her breakfast plate to the side. "It's true. You haven't been still since we sat down. Hanging your campaign posters around town this morning energized me too, but you're so antsy I'm about to write you a prescription for lisdexamfetamine. What's wrong?"

The weight of her friends' scrutiny made her want to shift in her seat, but she realized what she was doing and stopped. "Nothing. It's just…" Her fingers gravitated to a small tear in her napkin and proceeded to pull off a narrow strip of the flimsy paper.

Melody reached across the table and stilled her hand. "Oh my God. Stop shredding your napkin and talk."

"All right. Fine." She looked over her shoulder and scanned the half-empty diner. The Saturday brunch crowd hadn't hit DeShay's yet. Nobody was close enough to overhear. "It happened again."

Melody's eyes widened. She gasped, "No way," at the same time Ellie shook her head and said, "*What* happened again?"

"You and Wolverine?"

LouAnn leaned in. "Who's Wolverine?"

Ginny took a long sip of water rather than touch *that* question.

"We don't know," Melody said. "The new guy. Dark hair. Dangerous eyes. You've seen him around town."

"Oh," Ellie said. "You mean Shaun Buchanan?"

Ginny nearly spit out her water. "How did you know who he was?"

The brunette shrugged. "I remember him from elementary school."

"He looks completely different. How in God's name could you possibly have recognized him?"

"He resembles his mom, and she resembled my mom a little, which is no surprise because they were cousins. I guess the DNA tipped me off."

And there it was. Ellie's mom had died in a car accident shortly after Ellie's fourth birthday. Little Ellie, being scary-smart and missing her mama, had memorized the family tree and apparently imprinted the features of everyone in town who shared a branch or two.

"Plus he contacted Tyler to get a roof quote. He's fixing up a hunting cabin the family owns just outside of town."

"Time out," Melody interjected. "Are we talking Shaun Buchanan, as in Tom Buchanan's son?"

Ginny closed her eyes and nodded.

"Holy shit."

Holy shit, indeed. News had to be positively shocking to coax a swear word out of Melody Merritt, former Miss Bluelick, and poster child for southern manners.

LouAnn rubbed her forehead. "I'm confused. What happened between you and Shaun Buchanan?"

There was no getting out of this gracefully. And why bother? Melody was engaged to Josh, the man responsible for fueling the firefighter fantasies of every female in Bluelick old enough to play with matches. Ellie was engaged to Tyler Longfoot, a man who had sweet talked his way into the panties of scores of women between Bluelick and the state line—and you could identify them to this day by the satisfied smiles that split their faces when someone mentioned his name. LouAnn and Junior Tillman had been playing magnets for the better part of ten years—clicking together or pushing each other away, depending on how things lined up. None of the ladies were strangers to the power of amazing chemistry to make a normally level-headed woman behave like an idiot. Their houses boasted a bit too much glass for any of them to hurl stones at her.

She cleared her throat and quickly summarized for Ellie and LouAnn how a simple shave and haircut two nights ago had brought her sex hiatus to a shattering end.

"Wow." Ellie fanned her cheeks. "I can't believe you're

still feeling it two days later… Oh my God…did you"—she lowered her voice to a whisper—"Chapter Thirteen?"

Ginny laughed. Over a round at Rawley's a few nights ago to unofficially celebrate Ellie's engagement, she had confessed to them that she'd once ordered *The Wild Woman's Guide to Sex* in an effort to enhance her skills and seduce Melody's ex-fiancé, Roger. Of course, she'd ended up falling for Tyler instead, even though he flat-out refused to Chapter Thirteen her.

"Ellie, sweetie, your *Wild Woman* authors would have to come up with a whole bunch of new chapters to cover things that man and I got up to—no pun intended."

"I wonder if Tyler would Chapter Thirteen me if I gave him a shave and a haircut?"

"When you're engaged to a man with a nickname like 'Footlong Longfoot', you might want to settle for two Chapter Fives followed by a nice Chapter Three to finish things off," LouAnn observed. "Otherwise, you'll join the ranks of fidgety-pants over here, who can't sit still through breakfast."

Ellie eyed Ginny, and slowly nodded. "Maybe you're right."

"Let's get back to the Shaun Buchanan part." LouAnn tapped the table with a zebra-striped acrylic fingernail. "At what stage during your Thursday night sex-fest did he drop his last name and clue you in to the fact you were sleeping with the enemy?"

"Hey," Melody interjected, and narrowed her eyes at Ginny. "We went running the next day, and you told me you didn't know his last name."

"I didn't. Not then. Last night I stayed late at the salon to finish up some paperwork. When I left, I surprised some delinquent in the process of spray-painting a rude word on the wall of my shop. He bolted, and knocked me over like a bowling pin in the process."

"Good Lord, girl, are you all right?" LouAnn's hand landed on her arm and held on.

"I'm fine. I'd barely hit the sidewalk when Shaun appeared out of nowhere and ran the guy off. Then he convinced me to call the sheriff's department, and sat with me while some deputy named Bob Crocker pretended to give a shit."

"Yes, I've heard the sheriff's department's protect-and-serve skills leave something to be desired. Still, I'm glad you called it in," Ellie said. "At least they'll have the report."

"I think it was a waste of time. Crocker just kept harping on how I couldn't identify the guy, nor could Shaun. I finally snapped and told him I didn't have to see the guy to know who it was."

"Don't hold out on us. Who was it?" Melody squeezed her arm.

"Oh, come on, who would paint the word 'firecrotch' on the wall outside my salon, the same day I inform City Hall I'm running for mayor? I'll give you one guess."

Melody turned her hand palm up as if to say *I don't know*, but then smacked her forehead instead. "Justin."

"Right. Unfortunately, I can't prove it, and Crocker didn't believe me at all. He basically accused me of pointing the finger at Justin as a way to discredit Tom and get an advantage in the election. He turned to Shaun and said something like, 'Do you share Miss Boca's suspicions about your brother?' And *that's* how I found out I'd broken my sex hiatus with none other than Shaun Buchanan."

"Oops," Ellie said.

"Yeah, oops. I laid into him for not telling me who he was, and he fought back by saying he didn't know I was running for mayor, but basically calling me delusional if I believed knowing his last name would have made any difference the other night."

"Cocky," Melody noted.

"Very. But I can be cocky, too, so *I* told *him* it made a big freaking difference from here on out, and there would be no repeats."

Ellie's brows drew together. "But…didn't you start this conversation saying 'It happened *again*?'"

She felt her cheeks heat and sipped her water before continuing. "'Fraid so. This morning Shaun interrupted my morning run, hauled me into the Gas 'n Go restroom, and proceeded to make me come so hard I had to crawl home."

"Sweet baby Jesus in the manger." Melody practically crossed herself. "I hate when that happens. No, wait…I love when that happens."

"Yeah, but I know it's stupid of me to let it keep happening. I didn't know who he was that first night, so I can blame my weak moment on hormones. I don't have the same excuse for what happened this morning. There are so many reasons why I shouldn't be jumping the man. I don't know why my good sense disappears as soon as he touches me."

Ellie cleared her throat. "There's a medical term for the phenomenon. It's called 'screwing your brains out.'"

Ginny sat back in the booth and blew a stray hair off her face. "Well, I need the cure, or I'm going to look like a hypocrite, telling everyone in town we don't need the Buchanans while I've secretly got one stashed in my bed. Worse, I'll look like a manipulative bitch, trying to get the inside track on Tom's campaign by cozying up to his son."

"Sorry. Despite medical advances, there's no tried-and-true cure."

"That's not very helpful. I can't afford to let this…whatever it is…between Shaun and me happen again."

"You think he'll say something?" Melody asked.

"Shaun? No." She stared out the window at the gray clouds rolling in from the East. They were in for a soaking later. "I can't even pretend to know his deal, but I know he won't say a word. He's very…self-contained, and he's not looking to discredit me. His father and his brother, though? I can't say the same about them."

"But, if he's going to keep your secret"—Ellie turned her hands so her palms faced up, and looked around—"where's the risk?"

"You've been away so long you've forgotten how small towns work, but nobody knows better than a former gossip queen how impossible it is to keep a secret in Bluelick."

Her table-mates met the observation with silence. So that was that. She knew what she said was true, but had harbored a small hope the girls would point out some error in her logic.

LouAnn cleared her throat. "Want me to have Junior swing by the salon this afternoon and take care of your wall?"

"Thanks, but there's no need. Apparently, in addition to knowing how to keep a secret, Shaun knows how to paint. When I got to the salon this morning the graffiti was gone."

"Aww. That was sweet of him."

Yeah, so sweet she'd almost teared up right there on

the sidewalk. Not good. She didn't blush, and she didn't get misty-eyed over a sweet gesture. And yet, thanks to Shaun, she'd done both.

The diner door opened and Tom walked in with Ed Pinkerton, the manager of the hardware store. They headed toward a booth in the back, but Tom caught sight of her as they passed and detoured to their table.

"My esteemed opponent," he said loud enough to turn the rest of the heads in the diner their way.

"Hey Tom," she replied.

"I heard about your trouble last night at the hair parlor."

"Word travels fast."

"I keep my ear to the ground, especially when someone accuses my boy of wrongdoing."

She should have known that detail from last night would make it back to Tom at warp speed. *Especially since it only had one generation to travel.* The sharp-edged thought cut through her mind. Shaun had raced to her rescue last night—no argument—but why wouldn't his loyalties ultimately line up with his family? Then again, Crocker was just as likely the source. Or even Trent. Everybody knew Tom was in tight with the sheriff's department. It wouldn't be the first time they'd given him a heads-up about Justin.

No matter how the news got to Tom, the cold, hard, and very bitter reality was she had to watch what she said. She shoved her sense of betrayal aside, because Tom was in her face now, and she needed to deal with him, not try to figure out who'd stuck the knife in her back. This wasn't exactly how she envisioned entering into her first public debate, but Tom put the Justin issue out there, and she wasn't about to back down.

"Maybe you should get your ear off the ground and keep your eye on your kid instead?"

A few people behind her snickered.

Tom straightened to his full height, aligned his tie, and she became painfully aware he was standing over her like a principal with a disobedient schoolgirl.

"You're new to politics, Ginny, so I'll give you some advice. Free. There's a legal term for defaming a person with a false statement. It's called slander, and it will land you on the wrong end of a very expensive court judgment."

Was he filing a lawsuit? Her heart rattled in her chest and her palms grew damp at the thought of hiring a lawyer and spending thousands of dollars defending herself over one hastily spoken accusation, but letting him smell her fear would be the same as conceding defeat, so she raised her chin and returned his stare. "Thanks for the advice Tom. I've always been a little fuzzy on when something is libel and when it's slander, but I know one thing for certain."

"What's that?"

"Truth is an absolute defense."

"You don't have one shred of proof against Justin."

"Yet."

Tom shook his finger at her. "You've been warned. The next time you disparage my family, I'll see you in court."

Satisfied with the ultimatum, he turned and continued to his table. Silence reigned in the diner for several seconds, and then a low hum of conversation rushed in to fill the void.

Ginny exhaled and turned to LouAnn, Melody and Ellie. They stared back at her like she'd sprouted a second head. "What?"

"You're good," Melody said.

Ellie nodded. "My stomach's in a knot over here, but you stayed calm and sharp and you held your own. Tom walked away sputtering threats like a whiny crybaby."

"I appreciate the vote of confidence, but what you can't see is my stomach's in a knot, too. This little interaction drove two things straight home. First and foremost, I've got to watch my big mouth, or it's going to land me in court."

"What's the other?" LouAnn asked.

"I need to stay far away from Shaun Buchanan if I want to win this election."

Chapter Eight

If you're so intent on staying out of the local battles, why the hell do you keep putting yourself in the line of fire?

Shaun's caustic inner voice berated him as he strode down Main Street toward the salon, lugging the four foot fiberglass step ladder he'd borrowed from the cabin in one arm and carrying his toolbox and a nondescript black shopping bag in the other. Although it was barely five o'clock, storm clouds darkened the sky, throwing downtown into an early dusk. Thunder rumbled in the distance. He quickened his pace, and reached the salon just as a tiny, white-haired lady opened the door from the inside. After leaning the ladder against the wall, he grabbed the handle and held the door for her.

She squinted up at him through thick, frameless glasses, and smiled. "Thank you, sonny. Then she called over her shoulder, "Ginny, dear, I think you have a customer."

"What did you say, Ms. Van Hendler?" Ginny called

from the back of the salon. A second later she appeared around the corner, drying her hands on a towel. She stopped short at the sight of him.

He didn't miss the way her eyes narrowed, but the older lady continued talking, oblivious to the undercurrent of tension. "Though I must say, his hair looks just fine. I don't think he needs a trim." She lowered her voice to a not-very-soft whisper. "Maybe he wants some…what do you call it"—she turned and assessed him—"manscaping?"

Okay, yes, he was a mission-hardened SEAL, but every soldier had his breaking point, and he might have paled at the thought of having his body hair slathered in hot wax and ripped out at the roots.

"Ms. V," Ginny admonished, and the deceptively sweet-looking woman laughed.

"Just a guess, dear." She shifted her owl-eyes back to him and grinned. "I don't know what you young folks are into these days, with all the tattoos and body piercings and what-have-you, but I imagine it takes quite a bit of grooming."

"Ah. No, I'm good."

"I'll bet you are, sonny." She winked and walked out the door he still held open. He turned and headed in, nearly dropping his tools when he felt a quick but unmistakable squeeze in a personal zone.

He waited until the door clicked shut behind him. "Did she just pinch my ass?"

Ginny's shrug was non-committal. "You have to watch Ms. V. She's more plugged in than she lets on." She leaned against the reception counter and folded her arms, as if to dispel any notion her comment represented solidarity of any sort. The silent message reached him loud and clear. *I'm keeping my distance.* "What are you doing here, Buchanan?"

She used his last name only. Summed him up and damned him in a single word. He aimed to prove her wrong. "You have a problem I can solve."

Her brows shot up. "I do?"

As an answer, he put his toolbox down on the floor and held out the shopping bag.

She eyed the bag like it might contain a live rattler. "I've been solving my own problems for a long time."

"Okay. I'll just leave this with you, then." He pushed the bag into her hands. "Instructions are inside." Hoping she didn't call his bluff, he reached for his tools, and bit back a smile when curiosity got the better of her and she peeked in the bag. A 'v' formed between her brows, and then she reached into the bag and pulled out a small, round device.

"What's this?"

"That, sweet Virginia, is a state-of-the-art, motion sensitive, night-vision-enabled HD surveillance cam. I could have gone with something larger and more visible, if your goal was to deter your graffiti artist, but I figured you wanted to catch the bastard, not force him to get creative."

She stared at him for a moment, seemingly at a loss for words. Then she looked back at the camera resting in the palm of her hand. "It's so…small."

"Professional grade. If something triggers the motion detector, the digital camera will record and send the video to your phone. A friend of mine is kind of an expert on this type of thing, and he helped me pick it out. He also assured me it's easy to set up. I'm sure someone so adept at solving her own problems will have no difficulty, but"—he tapped his toolbox—"I've got my tools and some time, if you want me to handle the install."

She dropped the camera into the bag and handed it to him. His heart lightened when she rested her hand on his chest. "Sorry I acted like a bitch. I can't believe you thought to do this, and I'd be incredibly grateful if you'd install the dang thing for me. Thank you."

He resisted the urge to move into her touch, because it was an unconscious gesture of gratitude, not a come-on. Plus, if he decided to push his luck, the installation might be delayed for hours. "You're welcome. I'm going to get the camera positioned before it starts raining."

"I can help. Hand you tools, or—?"

"No." He pushed the door open and paused there to admire her, all slim legs and glowing skin in cuffed, white shorts and a slouchy, pink, shoulder-revealing top. Whenever she moved, the wide V-neck offered a peek at her subtle cleavage, snug in some lace-trimmed white thing she wore beneath. She raised an arm to run her fingers through her hair, and the sleeve went sliding. He had a sudden desire to lick her from the point of her shoulder to the tips of her toes, with plenty of detours along the way.

Thunder boomed aggressively in the silence, breaking into the moment they were having. She blinked, and he got the distinct impression he hadn't been the only one contemplating detours, especially when her cheeks turned almost as pink as her shirt. "Okay, then. I'm going to…um…finish cleaning up." She spun and bee-lined to the back of the salon.

He gave himself another moment to admire her flustered retreat, not to mention her tight little ass in the white shorts, and then stepped out on the sidewalk and got to work.

Installing the camera didn't take long. He mounted it to the base of the carriage-style fixture that hung over the door, so the wrought-iron and frosted glass obscured the lens from any eagle-eyed onlookers. A flip of a switch, the camera's green "active" light came on, and down he went.

Back inside he followed the instructions to download the monitoring app to his phone, and then hers, while she sat beside him, uncharacteristically quiet. Over the occasional rumble of thunder, he could practically hear her warring with herself about whether to ask the questions on the tip of her tongue, and figured it was only a matter of time before curiosity won out. Three…two…

"Where'd you learn how to do this?"

"It's amazing what you pick up during six years with the SEALs."

"So, surveillance was your area of expertise?"

"No." He hit the new icon on his phone and pulled up the view from the camera outside. He showed it to her. "I'm going to program the scan area a little tighter to the wall, because you don't want an alert every time someone walks past your shop."

"Sounds reasonable," she replied, but he could tell by her cautious tone she hadn't missed the fact that he'd dodged her inquiry. He zoomed in and adjusted the setting, feeling her eyes on him the entire time.

For some inexplicable reason, he found himself circling back to her question. "I have a friend in Cincinnati who also used to be with the SEALs. He's the technical guy. I went to see him today, explained what I needed, and he hooked me up with the cameras."

"Ah. Well, I really appreciate you doing this. Can I

reimburse you for the equipment? I have no idea how much stuff like this runs, but—"

"Don't worry about it. He owed me a favor."

She hesitated. He looked up from the phone screen and held her gaze, so she could see he meant what he said, but ended up lost in her clear green eyes. Finally her eyelids dropped down and her mouth tipped up at one corner. "All right. Thank you."

"You're welcome."

"I also noticed someone painted over the graffiti, and I really appreciate it."

"Somebody has a lot of flexibility in his schedule right now."

"Did you...?" She trailed off and he sensed the war going on in her head again.

"Did I what?"

"Did you talk to your father about last night, by any chance?"

The question surprised him. He wasn't sure why she asked, but he didn't need a map to know he was walking into a minefield. Still, in he went, because that's where she wanted to go.

"No. I drove to the house last night to talk to him, or Justin, or both, but Brandi was the only one home. I asked her to tell Tom to call me, but that's about as effective as asking a housecat to relay a message. I was in Cincinnati all day today, so I've been out-of-pocket."

"Oh." Her single-word response didn't give away much, but she rolled her shoulders and tipped her head to one side.

"Why do you ask?"

She tipped her head to the other side, working out some

invisible kink, and he imagined his hand there, at the base of her neck, slowly massaging the stiffness from her muscles. Then she sighed and said, "I'm sorry. I shouldn't have asked. What goes on between you and your father is none of my business, and I don't intend to make what goes on between me and him any of your business."

"Of course not. What went on between you and Tom?"

That earned him a quick laugh. "I just told you, it's none of your business."

"I'm a highly trained combat specialist. I have ways of making you talk."

"Ha. I'll bet you do. But your ways are not going to work on me. I made a pact with myself to be more circumspect, especially after last night. I shouldn't have told Crocker Justin spray-painted my wall when I had no proof."

He agreed, but simply shrugged rather than second the conclusion. "You think he did it."

"I *know* he did it, but making an accusation against Justin, under the circumstances, amounts to making an accusation against Tom, and stuff like that could come back and bite me if I can't prove it. I'm also sorry for putting you in an awkward position last night. Justin's your brother—"

"You didn't put me in any kind of position." He interrupted her to make the point because this was the second "sorry" to come out of her mouth for something she had no reason to feel sorry about. "If I'd been able to identify the guy, I would have done so, regardless of whether it was Justin or Moses or God himself. I don't know who it was, but if he does an encore, we're going to nail his ass." He held up her phone. "You ready to see how?"

She nodded and took it from him.

He walked her through the app. When he finished, he stepped outside and tested the camera, which served as a half-decent test of the night-vision capabilities thanks to the premature darkness from the incoming storm. Everything worked. They both received the alert. She accessed the video on her phone and whistled at the resolution.

"This is light years ahead of the grainy convenience store videos you see on the news every once in a while. Why doesn't everybody have these?"

His silence brought her head up. She searched his face. "Exactly how big was this favor your friend owed you?"

"Bigger than a convenience store security camera."

She drew in a deep breath. He watched the sleeve of her pink shirt slide down her arm again. His hand twitched with an impulse to reach out and brush the thin strap of the white top off her shoulder as well.

"I noticed two cameras in your bag of tricks."

He forced his gaze back to her face, and kept his expression deliberately neutral, because he didn't want her realizing the calling card her unknown artist had left last night bothered him more than cruder messages might have. It struck him as targeted, and personal, and not necessarily the work of a spoiled teen with a chip on his shoulder and a warped sense of family loyalty. "I thought you might want one for your house. Invite me over and I'll install it for you."

Her eyes evaded his while she worried her lower lip with her teeth. "I appreciate the offer, but I can't accept. If my neighbors saw your Jeep in front of my house, tongues would wag. I can't risk the speculation right now…especially with you…"

He couldn't risk the chance of her surprising her graffiti

artist on her doorstep instead of at the salon. "I'll park down the street and walk up." The words tasted only slightly bitter in his mouth. "Nobody will know I'm there."

Thunder cracked overhead like a warning shot.

. . .

Rain battered Ginny's windshield as she steered her Ford Escape down Main Street past the fire station and made a left at the first intersection after the square. In her rearview mirror she watched the headlights behind her make the turn as well. She'd bought the Escape because it was roomy and maneuverable, but now, as she led Shaun to her house, she wondered if she ought to hit the gas and do as the car's name suggested.

Hello, sane Ginny to crazy Ginny. Come in crazy Ginny. Did you not just swear this guy off at breakfast today?

Yes she had. But then he'd showed up at her salon and seduced her with fancy surveillance equipment. Not to mention the way he handled his tools. He was one of those guys who sank a screw with quick, efficient twists of his wrist. No fuss, no fumbling.

Plus, he hadn't told Tom what she'd said about Justin.

Which meant her first instinct…well…second instinct, had been right. Somebody at the sheriff's department fed Tom information. Predictable. He supported the department wholeheartedly, and Crocker was probably one of his cronies. She wasn't the first citizen to suggest Bluelick might fare better with its own police department, but Tom always argued against it. Sheriff Butler appeared more than willing to return Tom's loyalty.

A few blocks down Union, the historic brick townhomes separated into Colonials and Victorians with gracefully down-sloping front yards. The road angled up a hill, and the bigger homes transitioned to smaller houses from the 1930s and 1940s dotting the steeper hillside. A tidy, well-tended working class neighborhood rather than a fancy one, but it suited her fine.

She slowed as her broad, white garage came into view, and hit the clicker to raise the door. As she pulled in, she saw the Wrangler drive past. Her hero, once again coming to her rescue.

What are you going to do with this man?

All kinds of interesting ideas formed in her mind, but then a fit of paranoia gripped her. Would neighbors see him coming up to her house and draw conclusions? Ms. Van Hendler lived a few doors down, and despite the impression the octogenarian liked to give people, she didn't miss much. Then again, the hard rain made it unlikely anyone would be taking an evening walk. And it wasn't like he'd be there all night. Right?

She reached around and grabbed the large umbrella from her backseat, and then squeezed out her driver's side door. A few side-steps took her around her car, and then she watched in dry-mouthed wonder as Shaun walked up her driveway, wet hair shoved back from his face, rain-drenched gray U.S. Navy T-shirt clinging to every hard line of his shoulders and chest. His eyes locked on her like a predator mesmerizing its prey.

A shiver ran down her spine, and she blamed the involuntary reaction on the drop in temperature brought on by the storm. He stopped just inside the garage, blinked the raindrops off his eyelashes, and focused on her. "Lead the way."

"Yes, um…okay." She kicked her butt into gear and walked to the side door of her garage. She felt more than heard him behind her, and touched the button on the wall that lowered the automatic door. They stepped out of the garage, and she did her best to cover them both with her umbrella as they navigated the steep, carved-stone steps leading to her front door. Silly, considering he was already soaked to the skin, and their height difference made it far more likely she'd poke out his eye than shield him from the rain, but some deep-seated part of her felt compelled to offer him shelter, even if he didn't seem to want it.

When they reached her covered porch, she propped the umbrella against the rail and searched through her purse for her keys. From the corner of her eye she saw him put his toolbox down and set the bag beside it.

"I can put the camera up here." He pointed to the light hanging from the porch ceiling above them. "That will get film of anyone who comes near your door."

"Sounds like a plan." She unlocked her door and pushed it open, flipped on the outside light then looked back at him, surprised to see him heading down the steps.

"Where are you going?"

"To my car, to get the ladder."

"No need. I have a step-stool. Come on in. I'll grab it."

He climbed the three steps back onto her porch and ran his hand through his hair, pushing wet strands off his forehead. Then he inspected the mud caked in the tread of his thick soled work boots. "I'll wait out here."

She rolled her eyes, but didn't bother wasting her breath

to argue her interior could stand up to a little mud. Instead she slipped out of her pink ballet flats and left them on her welcome mat to dry. Her bare feet slapped against the old pine floors as she hurried down the hall to the linen closet and grabbed a towel. She swung through her kitchen on the way back to get the fold-up stool she kept tucked in the gap between the fridge and the wall.

By the time she returned to the porch, he had a flashlight and his tools set out in a neat line on the rail and the camera unpackaged. Efficient. He reached out to take the step-stool from her, but she handed him the towel instead. "Here. Dry off first."

He stared at the towel like it was a foreign object for a moment, during which time she realized she'd just offered him the Ariel beach towel her crazy aunt Jackie had sent her after taking a trip to Orlando, because…well…redhead. When she looked up at him, she caught the telltale twitch of his lip.

"It was a *gift*. My aunt thinks I look like The Little Mermaid."

His eyes shifted from her to the cartoon on the towel, and then back at her. "Your aunt has a point. Thanks, Ariel."

She meant to set up the step-stool while he dried off, but the sight of him roughing the towel over his hair, his face, and then dragging it down his chest and abs derailed her intentions. She imagined standing with him under the soft glow of the porch light, helping him pull the wet shirt over his head, and then running the towel all over his bare, damp skin. Her attention drifted to his rain-splattered jeans. In her mind's eye she knelt before him and slowly undid the buttons at his fly, pushed his jeans down his long, powerful legs, and then…

A towel appeared in her line of vision, blocking out her fantasy. She blinked, took the towel, and raised her eyes to his.

"Thank you, sweet Virginia," he said, but his not-so-innocent smile suggested he wasn't thanking her for the towel so much as the impure thoughts. Heat seeped into her face and there wasn't a damn thing she could do about it.

"No problem," she muttered, and strode into the house, but after a few restless minutes puttering around in the kitchen, she gave up trying to distract herself and wandered back out to the porch. This time she made herself useful, running to the breaker box in the little utility room just inside her back door, and turning off the power to the porch light at his signal. Then she was back, sharing the step-stool with him, trying to ignore the heat coming off his body as she held the flashlight so he could see what he was doing.

He smelled like soap, and rain, and testosterone. His jaw flexed as he screwed the base of the camera to the wooden slats of her porch ceiling. A stray drop of water ran down his neck and disappeared under the collar of his shirt. Her tongue itched to follow the wet trail.

"Okay," he said softly, and for a moment she thought he was giving her permission to run her tongue over his skin, but then he lowered his arms and added, "want to go flip the switch?"

Oh yeah. That. "Absolutely. Sure." She handed him the flashlight and practically jumped off the stool. "Be right back."

She hustled to the breaker box and threw the switch, then inched down the hall far enough to confirm the light flickered on. From the porch she heard him utter something that sounded like, "Lightning knows his shit," which she took to mean the camera worked. She stopped in the kitchen to pour a glass of water, briefly considered throwing it over her head to cool herself down, but settled for a deep drink before she returned to the porch.

He stood there bathed in porch light, with his head tipped down and his eyes closed, absently rubbing the back of his neck. God, he looked…weary. Just like the night she'd dragged him into her salon and watched his eyelids grow heavy as she chatted his ear off and trimmed his hair. A bunch of stupid and highly misplaced protective instincts rose up and took control of her mouth.

She ran a hand down his back, feeling his body heat through the drenched T-shirt. "Have you had dinner?"

He straightened and looked at her. "I planned to pick up something from Boone's on the way home."

"Change your plan. I'll make dinner."

Now he started gathering up his tools. "I don't want to track up your house. I'm all dirty and wet."

It was on the tip of her tongue to say, "Me, too," but she swallowed the wayward retort. "Not a problem. Leave your shoes by the door and you won't track up my house. You can shower while I get dinner ready, and I'll toss your clothes in the dryer."

"I don't want to put you to any trouble."

"Tell you what, I'll save the coq au vin for another night, but I have this funny habit of eating every evening, and I can just as easily boil up a whole box of pasta as half."

The sarcasm earned her a smile. He closed the lid on his toolbox. "Well, when you put it like that…"

"I put it exactly like that." She waited while he unlaced his boots, slipped them off and left them neatly paired up by her door. Her shoes looked ridiculously small and delicate — and strangely intimate — resting beside his.

But it wasn't until he stepped into her entryway that she fully appreciated the meaning of the word intimate. He took up all room in the narrow space. The soft, sage green paint she'd painstakingly layered onto thick plaster walls seemed to nudge them together and the original etched glass fixture gracing the entryway dappled them in soft light. The steady pitter-patter of rain on the roof insulated her ears from mundane noises like the tick of her grandma's mantle clock in the living room, or the hum of the refrigerator kicking on in the kitchen.

Dirty, wet, and tired, she reminded herself, and led him down the hall to the one and only bathroom, stopping at the built-in linen closet to dig out another towel. She chose a blue striped one this time.

"No mermaid?"

"I'm sorry. Did you *want* a mermaid towel?"

He shrugged. "Might be the closest I get to showering with a redhead tonight."

Chapter Nine

Shaun braced his hands on the blue-tiled shower wall, tipped his head down and let the hot water beat down on his scalp. He attempted a turn in the tiny compartment and smacked his elbow into the frosted glass door. The flimsy latch gave, the door flew open and water doused the white bathmat. He pulled the door shut so he could finish rinsing off without flooding the small room. Damn it, pre-war bathrooms weren't built for guys his size. This was like showering in a doll house.

The space seemed even smaller thanks to all the girl stuff closing in on him from every available surface. His showers up until now had been blissfully devoid of salts, muds, butters, brushes, and other junk populating Ginny's bathroom. He slid the soap from the stingy, yet overflowing, built-in shelf and was about to scrub it across his chest when something made him stop and sniff the plain, white bar. The sweet, sunny scent of Virginia snuck into his nostrils, infiltrated his nervous system, and tugged hard on his dick. As much as he appreciated the effect, the idea of walking around smelling like a honey-dipped lemon blossom gave him pause. But he figured *she'd* appreciate it more than him walking around smelling like sweat and rain. He lathered up and imagined her in there with him, her wet hair streaming like liquid fire over her pale skin. He practically felt her soap-slicked hands sliding along his neck, down his back, and then sneaking around front to cup his balls. His eyelids drooped while his cock sprang to life. Finally, those slim fingers would curl around his—

The soap slipped out of his hand and landed with a thud on the tile floor. When he bent over to get it, his ass hit the shower door. The latch gave out again and this time the door flew open so hard it slammed into the bathroom wall. Water from the shower sprayed everywhere.

"Shit!"

He grabbed the door and pulled it closed. It clattered into the latch at the same time Ginny knocked on the door and called, "Is everything all right in there?"

"Fine," he called over the cascade of the shower. *Just standing here with a hard-on that won't back off, systematically demolishing your bathroom.*

"Okay. Take your time. Your jeans are dry. I'm just going to pop in and leave them for you."

He stared through the frosted glass as her blurry outline moved into his line of sight. She put his folded jeans on the counter, puttered around with something or other by the sink, and then turned. He couldn't tell for sure, but he got the impression she was staring at the shower.

"Do you…have everything you need?" The hesitant,

husky voice encompassed him as completely as the warm steam from the shower. Her palm formed a dark shadow on the glass door.

No. I need you to strip down, get in here, and... Some scrap of pride wouldn't let him say the words though. Virginia wasn't a hesitant girl, but she had plenty of hesitations about him. Being her impulsive mistake, yet again, didn't sit well with him. "I'm good. Thanks." If she wanted more, she was going to have to say so, without hesitation or the escape hatch of "one last time."

"Great. Good." The shadow of her hand disappeared. "I'll go start dinner."

The *thunk* of the bathroom door told him she'd left. He turned off the water, listened to her footsteps continue down the hall, and tried not to be disappointed. He shouldn't be, he told himself as he dried off and pulled on his briefs and jeans. She had her goals, and spending time with him put one of the main ones at risk. Meanwhile, his life needed a few fundamentals—little stuff like some goddamned direction and a new career—before he started layering in distractions. And even if he was settled enough to consider a relationship, his father's adversary would be an inadvisable choice—for all of them.

Valid points, but they didn't do much for the disappointment. He made his way down the hall toward the kitchen, barefoot and shirtless, serenaded by the sound of Ginny half-singing, half-humming. He stepped into the kitchen and saw her.

Part of her, anyway. She was bent over, with her head in the oven, presenting him with a stunning view of her backside covered by those innocent white shorts.

"Ginny."

She looked over her shoulder at him, smiling. "I think that's the first time you've called me—" But as she took in the sight of him standing there her words trailed off and the smile disappeared.

"I hope this isn't one of those no shoes, no shirt, no services places."

The smile snuck back to her lips. She straightened and closed the oven. "No. We're pretty casual here at Casa Boca. Can I get you a beer or something?"

Alcohol had turned into a hazard as soon as his sleep problems had started, but it was one he'd been smart enough to recognize and avoid. "I'm fine. I'm no Anthony Bourdain, but I can stir a pot or—"

She waved his offer off. "Everything's under control. I put the game on in the sitting room. Go on in, relax, and take a load off. I'll call you when dinner's ready."

He wasn't sure if she was trying to indulge him or get him out of her hair, but either way, the idea of kicking back for a few minutes suddenly sounded pretty damn good. A few steps down the hall brought him to her sitting room. The lighting was low, and mainly from the television. Springs in the dark blue sofa squeaked as he sat. He moved a fancy, fringed decorative pillow off to the side, and fingered the fluffy, matching throw draped over the back of the sofa. Girl stuff—as fascinating as it was confounding.

He slung an arm along the sofa back and stared at the screen. Seventh inning shut-out. The remote sat on the dark, mission-style coffee table in front of him. He picked it up, intending to channel surf, but ended up just turning the volume down and leaving the game on.

Virginia's soft, smoky rendition of "Umbrella" drifted to him from across the hall. The images on the screen started to blur. He blinked them back into focus, once…twice…and then gave in to the compulsion to rest his eyes for five lousy minutes.

• • •

"Wake up, sleeping beauty."

Shaun jerked upright and looked around as if totally disoriented.

"Hey." She put her hand on his shoulder. "Ginny's house, camera install, thank you dinner, remember?"

"Yeah." He rubbed the heels of his hands over his eyes, and she suspected he wouldn't appreciate knowing how much he looked like a tired little boy, but the gesture transported her back in time, to an early memory. She couldn't have been more than four or five, sitting between her parents in a pew at Bluelick Baptist, watching young Shaun Buchanan several pews over, yawning and rubbing his eyes.

"You snuck in a nap." Hoping to tease the haunted expression from his face, she took a seat beside him on the sofa and added, "That's twice you've fallen asleep on me. I think I'm boring you."

"No." He shook his head. "It's not you. It's me. I… haven't been sleeping well." The words came out reluctantly, like the last drops of water from a dry well.

"You poor man. How long has this been going on?" She didn't know about anyone else, but her life went to hell in a hand-basket pretty damn quick if she dragged around more than a few days without a good night's sleep.

He stared at her for a long moment. "On and off for seven months."

"Seven months?" *Men.* "That's a ridiculous amount of time to suffer. Have you talked to a doctor?"

He opened his mouth to say something, but then expelled a breath and ran a restless hand through his hair, leaving it sticking up in the kind of haphazard disarray some guys spent lots of time and product trying to achieve. "I've talked the whole mess to death—with my commanding officer, my doctor—"

"Well, fine. Now talk to *me.*" She scooted closer when he edged away. He was feeling penned in? Too bad. People talked to her. That was her gift. "Talk to me," she repeated, never taking her eyes off his face.

His hand attacked his hair again, and then he dropped his arm, tilted his head back and closed his eyes. Surrender.

"My sleep problems started shortly after my last mission with the SEALs."

Her heart sank under a creeping wave of dread. Whatever came next was going to be bad. Not Justin-painted-a-foul-word-on-my-wall bad, or anything else that passed for bad in Bluelick, but the kind of fucked-up that messed with the head of one of the strongest of the strong. She took a fortifying breath, and pressed on. "Coincidence?"

His laugh contained absolutely no humor. "Not so much. My last mission went sideways, to put it mildly."

"Tell me."

He laughed again, and shook his head. "Trust me Virginia, you do not want to hear the details."

"Why? They're just words, Shaun. They can't hurt me... unless..." She lowered her voice to a dramatic whisper. "If you tell me, are you going to have to kill me?"

This time his laugh came closer to real amusement, and his eyes found hers. "If I said yes, would you drop the subject?"

"No. I'd take my chances. Where was your last mission?"

His eyes drifted away. "The Sudan. Counterterrorism mission involving a high-value target within Al-Qaeda. Go in. Extract him from the compound where he was living in plain sight under a false identity. Bring him to justice."

Jesus. She styled hair for a living. It suddenly seemed so ridiculous. "Sounds cut-and-dried," she deadpanned.

"It should have been. We got our intel from a reliable local informant. Satellite pictures confirmed everything he told us. Our target lived like a king in a fancy enclave on the outskirts of Khartoum, in a spacious home with a panoramic view of the Nile. Approximately seventy-five members of his family, staff, and aides lived there, too."

"Sounds like a lot of…variables."

"The SEALs are trained for variables. Part of the deal is to get the job done with precision. A good team can nab a feral rat from a Tokyo subway at rush hour without a single witness—if nothing goes wrong."

"But, in your case, something went wrong." Her stomach clenched at the thought, but she told herself to toughen up. This had been his reality. All she had to do was listen.

"The thing about informants in a place like the Sudan is they're poor. Poor at a level people in the U.S. can't fathom. They have poor parents, siblings, spouses and children, and they're all trying to survive any way they can. A family member learned what was going on and took the information to our target."

"Oh, no." The clench in her stomach evolved to a cramp.

"The night of the mission, we came in slightly off our timetable. High winds delayed our chopper about ten minutes. We'd barely breached the outer walls when the whole compound blew sky high. Our target was a firm believer in the scorched earth policy."

"God. Shaun." She couldn't stop herself from reaching for him, or stop the immediate sense of relief when his hand closed over hers and his warmth seeped into her skin. "Were you hurt?"

"Not a scratch. Not on me, or anybody else on the team. But there were casualties. Lots of them. Inside…" He trailed off and rubbed a hand over his forehead, as if to erase images lingering in his mind.

"I don't understand. If the guy blew up his own home, who would have been inside?"

"All of his wives, all of the daughters, and most of the domestic staff. The final body count came to forty-three."

"Good lord." A sick taste polluted the back of her throat. She rested her free hand on his shoulder and held on. "Why?"

He raised and lowered his shoulders in a matter-of-fact gesture. "You can disappear with a handful of sons and a few aides, but you can't empty an entire household without somebody noticing all the activity. So he cut his losses, left the rest of them there as unsuspecting bait, and hoped to take out a SEAL team at the same time. Even feral rats know a few tricks."

Her next question came from a hard, vengeful place inside her she never knew existed, and she couldn't ask it in a voice above a whisper. "Did you get the rat?"

He squeezed her hand. "Affirmative. We waded into that blown-out, burning shell of a building, over bodies of women and children in unimaginable condition, until we found a woman—one woman—crying her kids' names. She was in terrible shape…she was just…" He stopped, drew in a breath, and let it out slowly. "She wasn't going to make it. But she was alive, and conscious enough to understand her children weren't. And she gave our rat up. Told us exactly where to find him. We went. We found him. We completed our mission."

"And after?"

"After? I decided my rat hunting days were over. Continuing meant learning to accept the risk, if not responsibility, for extreme collateral damage. I worried getting comfortable with the risk might eventually make it difficult to separate the rats from, say, my own reflection."

"Shaun, you own no part of the responsibility for what some crazy extremist decided to do to evade justice."

"We set events in motion. The hindsight view provides an interesting landscape of what-ifs."

"What if your team never acted on the informant's tip? What if the next building the rat blew up was an office tower where thousands of innocent people worked, or a school, or—?"

"All good questions. I don't have the answers. I only have the what-ifs."

Hoping he'd keep talking, she stayed silent, but started massaging the bunched-up muscles in his shoulders.

He let out a low sigh, and leaned back into her touch. "For a long time afterwards, every time I closed my eyes I went straight back to that night. Sometimes half the team is inside when the building blows. Sometimes just me. Sometimes I'm rushing to get there because I know it's going to blow. I'm running balls out, using all my energy, but I'm not moving fast—I can't make any progress. Ever had a dream like that?"

"Yes." She offered the soft reassurance and kept soothing his shoulders. "It's common."

"The dream analysts say it means you can't outrun your problems."

"No, but you can share them. Want to know why you shared them with me tonight?"

The corners of his mouth tipped up into a tight grin. "Because you wouldn't shut up until I talked?"

"No." But she couldn't restrain a smile of her own. She could be persistent. "You told me because you need something I can give you."

The hint of a smile still lingered around his mouth. "What can you give me, sweet Virginia?"

Comfort, she thought. *I can give you comfort.* But strong, silent Shaun Buchanan wasn't the kind of man to accept sympathy if he saw it coming, so she leaned into him and placed a kiss on his lips. Then she slid her palms over his chest, down the dips and ridges of his torso, and into the waistband of his jeans.

"This."

Chapter Ten

"Let me."

Those two little words reached his ears at the same time her fingers reached the first button on the fly of his jeans. Then she kissed him—long, deep, and persuasive as hell. He brought his hand up to hold her head and invaded her sweet mouth. She sealed her lips around the base of his tongue and slowly sucked her way to the tip, wringing a shudder from him.

He broke away and buried his face in the curve of her neck. "Christ, Virginia."

"Sit back. Relax. Let me make you feel good."

He groaned, then closed his eyes, covered her hand with his, and moved it down the front of his jeans, loving the way she handled him. "You've made me feel good many times. A few of those occurred before we ever met."

Her hand stilled for a beat, before those slim fingers undid another button. "Did you think of me…touch yourself"—her voice brushed the skin along his throat like velvet—"and pretend it was me touching you?" She grasped him through the denim and squeezed his whole package harder than was strictly polite, but he loved the unapologetically straightforward demand. He couldn't feel anything except what she was doing to him.

Eyes closed, chin to chest, he breathed in her scent. "Fuck yes."

She popped the rest of the buttons in a series of quick, urgent tugs, and, at last, curled her fingers around his shaft. A starburst of lights twinkled behind his closed eyelids.

"How did you touch yourself? Gently?" Her diabolical fingertip took a slow, feather-light tour of the vein running along the underside of his cock.

He was literally incapable of answering, but it hardly mattered, because she didn't wait for a response.

"Or did you like it rough?" She tightened her grip on his shaft and worked him harder.

"Fast," he choked out in what was almost a laugh. "Since I didn't have company, I wasn't worried about lasting."

The confession pulled a slow, sexy grin out of her. She pressed her lips to his throat, the underside of his jaw, while she continued to stroke him. True, he wasn't in the same hard-up condition he'd been in a few weeks ago, but if she kept this up, the result wasn't going to be a hell of a lot different.

"Virginia—"

"No," she interrupted. "I'm doing all the work this time. You're going to sit back and endure it."

Not likely. He'd never been a sit-back kind of guy, but he stilled anyway. She tugged him free of his jeans and briefs. He looked down and enjoyed an unobstructed view of her slim, pale hand curled around the thickest part of him. His head jutted from the top of her fist.

"I'm going to take such good care of you, you're not going to be sure where your fantasies end and reality begins." So saying, she lowered herself to her knees in front of him and let her breath waft across the tip of his cock.

He groaned and gripped the base of his erection, just under her hand.

"You're going to drive me insane…oh, Jesus."

She cupped his balls at the same time she stroked him, stopping just shy of the flare of his head. "So, you're touching yourself, and thinking of me, and…"

His head dropped back of its own accord, and his breath quickened. "I'd dream of you kneeling between my legs, opening your mouth, and letting me fuck you like that until I was the only thing you'd taste for the rest of your life."

While they both watched, liquid beaded at the head of his cock and trembled there. He shivered when she used the pad of her thumb to swipe it, pressing down hard enough to explore the small opening. Then she brought her thumb to her mouth and licked it clean.

Eyes locked on him, she gripped his thighs, spreading them slightly, and brought her mouth so close her breath ruffled the hair around the base of his cock. "Could I trouble you to do the honors?"

Hell yes. He gripped his shaft and guided it to her lips. She opened her mouth, fully prepared to take him in, but he delayed their gratification by tracing his tip along her upper lip. "You have the softest lips, Virginia. Even before I ever kissed you, I knew they'd feel amazing." He dragged his tip along her lower lip and couldn't hold back a groan.

She chased him with her tongue, wetting her lips in the process. "Having them sealed around you is going to feel even better."

He placed his hand on the top of her head, spearing his fingers through her hair. "Don't rush me. This is my dream, remember?"

"I remember everything. Tell me what comes next."

Why he wanted to torture himself he couldn't say, but he wanted to savor this. "Kiss it…just the tip. With those plush lips of yours. No tongue, yet."

She wet her lips again, puckered them, and rubbed them over the tip he held out for her. Somehow he managed to keep his eyes open, even though they wanted to roll back in his head. Then she parted her lips to take him deeper.

"Not yet," he ground out, still hoping against hope to make this last more than three seconds.

"I can't wait. I want to cradle the weight of you in my mouth. I want to hear you beg as I take you in." She tightened her hold on his thighs and aimed a plaintive look at him.

"Sweet Virginia, you've got me so worked up I can't trust myself. If you let me in your mouth, I'm going to own it. I've been fantasizing about this too long to sit by like a gentleman while you have your fun."

"Do you think you're scaring me off?" She parted her lips as if in a dare, and ran her tongue along the same vein her fingertip had traced earlier.

Control. Snapped. He tightened his fingers in her hair, pulled her head back a fraction of an inch, and pushed his cock into her mouth. She sealed her lips tight around him, either to slow his entry, or to fully appreciate the size and shape of him.

He almost didn't care, but managed to rein in his movement anyway. She countered with deep, enthusiastic suction.

"Christ, you feel so good," he gasped, as the lightshow behind his eyelids flickered again. Realizing he'd relinquished his view of her, he forced his eyes open and stared at his lap.

Virginia rose onto her knees and changed the angle to take more. *Not yet.* He tightened his fingers in her hair, held her head still, and withdrew a few millimeters. She made an impatient sound and her hands tightened on his thighs. "A minute," he managed. "Give me a minute. Once I get going, I won't be able to savor this—the hug of your lips, or the heat of your mouth—because I'm going to go hard, and I'm going to go deep. So do us both a favor and give me a goddamn minute."

As it turned out, he didn't have a minute in him. His hips tightened and flexed of their own accord. With one hand twisted in her hair, and the other gripping the seat of the sofa, he thrust. It wasn't easy. Their position worked against him, but he couldn't sit still. She dug her fingernails into his legs, held on, and hummed her approval as he thrust deeper—all the way to the soft, snug cavern at the back of her throat. She lowered her head to take just a little more, and the edges of his vision went gray. He eased back and then surged upward again, reflexively, forcefully, in rapid succession. Some detached part of his brain warned him to take care, because he didn't want to make her jaw ache from the strain of holding him, but she wouldn't tolerate any restraint. She kept him sealed tight while her eager tongue explored every inch it could reach.

Oxygen became a critical thing. His heart hammered in his chest. His breaths quickened as his thrusts became faster and shallower. Somebody was talking. Rambling, incoherent nonsense reached his ears over the drum of his own pulse. Curses…prayers…he couldn't be sure. And then he lost the thread of it completely because she sucked hard on his cock and the tension gathering at the base of his spine coursed downward toward his balls.

Before he could draw another much-needed lungful of air and brace himself for what came next, she speared two fingers behind his sac and found the exact spot where the pressure concentrated. Ribbons of heat scorched a path straight up his shaft. Light exploded behind his eyes. A hand dislodged his from its death grip on the sofa, and deceptively delicate fingers threaded through his, holding fast as the orgasm tore through him.

Who knew he'd survive four years at Annapolis, six years as a SEAL, dozens of dangerous missions all over the globe, only to die in Bluelick with a smile on his face, his extremely grateful dick limp in his lap, and a gorgeous redhead completely at fault?

The feathery tickle of eyelashes against his chest suggested maybe his nervous system was still plugged into his brain. He pried his eyes open and watched as the redhead in question pressed a kiss to his pec, then his collarbone, and then his temple. He contemplated saying something… *Thank you? Give me five minutes and I'll return the favor?* But suddenly she stopped, buried her nose in his hair and sniffed.

"Why does your hair smell like my soap?"

He tucked himself back into his jeans and buttoned up.

"I don't want to shock you."

She drew back and gave him what he could only classify as a horrified look. "Oh, no. You didn't…"

"Your shampoo is pink and smells like an herb garden. I took the soap—"

"Body soap."

He shrugged to show her what he thought of the distinction. "I scrubbed it over my head, which happens to be attached to my body. Then I rinsed."

Her fingers sifted through his hair, as if assessing the damage. "Bar soap isn't chemically formulated for hair. It's going to leave the strands weighed down and lifeless."

"It's hair. It's already lifeless." He tucked her back against his side.

"Neanderthal," she grumbled, but settled into a comfortable position.

The sense of contentment subsided a little when she trailed her index finger across his chest, tracing the letters of his tattoo. Not that her touch didn't feel like heaven—it did—but questions wouldn't be far behind and he was talked out on the subject of his military service. A part of him couldn't believe he'd opened up like he had, simply because she'd asked him. The odd thing was he did feel better. Something about the unflinching way she handled the ugly mess he'd dumped on her—something beyond the amazingly restorative power of a great blowjob—made him feel almost… normal. He caught her hand and linked their fingers.

"The only easy day was yesterday?"

"It's an unofficial SEAL motto. I got dragged out for standard commemorative ink after my first mission." Ironically, the words had never really felt true until after his last.

"A bunch of us did the same thing after graduating from cosmetology school."

"Seriously?" He'd inspected every inch of her mouthwatering body and he never noticed a tattoo.

She gave his chest a playful swat. "Hell, no. The idea of lying still while someone stabs me repeatedly with a needle to shove ink into my dermis sounds like a cruel and unusual punishment."

"Depends on your definition of unusual, I suppose."

She smiled and rested her head on his shoulder. He could have sat there for days, in comfortable silence, listening to the rain patter on the roof, but for some screwed up reason he asked, "Why run for mayor?"

She let her head roll back so it rested against the couch. Their bodies didn't lose contact, but he no longer had her breasts resting against his chest or her thigh next to his. And that was a damn shame. "Do you really want to talk about this?"

"I wouldn't have asked if didn't want to know. Don't trust me with the truth?"

"No. I trust you. I'm just not sure this is a good topic for us."

"Why?"

She looked uncomfortable with the question, even though they both knew the answer. "Because your dad is my opponent."

"Despite my last name, I don't really have a horse in this race."

"How do you figure?"

"Because the cabin I'm staying in is outside the city limits. I'm not a Bluelick resident and, therefore, not eligible to vote."

"Huh. Funny how that worked out."

"Totally unplanned"—not that he was complaining—
"but as a consequence, I'm asking out of personal interest
only. Why run for mayor?"

She exhaled a long breath and turned her head to face
him. "I don't know if you remember Grandma Boca?"

He searched his memory for a face, but came up blank.
"No."

"No reason you would, but she played a big role in my
life. No pun intended," she added under her breath.

"Sorry?"

"Bad joke. Grandma was, well, larger than life. My mama
used to say she had a problem with her glands, but as I got
older, I realized she had an eating disorder. She was addicted
to food, which is a tough addiction to break because you
actually do have to eat. Her size made normal activities like
walking and riding in a car an ordeal. She couldn't just drive
down to Boone's Market to shop, or scoot over to Dalton's
Drugs to pick up a prescription, or even attend church. As
she got wider, her world got very narrow—about as narrow
as the four walls of my parents' home—and I became her
link to the rest of Bluelick. I loved my grandma and I didn't
want her to feel like she was missing out, so I made a point
to talk to people, and listen, and learn everything I could
about what was going on so I could share the news with her
when I got home."

Shaun imagined a teenaged Virginia talking with her
grandmother, bonding over all the shit he tried to avoid…
details about who was getting married, having babies,
achieving something, or suffering a setback. "I'm sure she

appreciated spending time with you, and the effort you took to make her feel included in everyday life."

"She did, but she also pushed me to do more than just relay the information. She asked for my thoughts, my opinions, and my solutions. I can still hear her saying, 'Peanut, if you were in this person's shoes, what would you do?'"

"Peanut, huh?"

She narrowed her eyes and aimed her finger at him. "I've let you get away with calling me Virginia. Do *not* press your luck unless you're ready to sacrifice a couple nuts of your own."

He couldn't fathom why the threat of having his balls torn off made him smile, but it did. "You were saying, Virginia?"

"I was saying Grandma B encouraged me to think about people's problems, and what I could do to help. I mean, don't get me wrong, she enjoyed a juicy piece of gossip as much as the next person—maybe more—but along with that, she had genuine concern and compassion, and a lack of patience for people who sat around complaining about a problem rather than trying to solve it. She always urged me to get involved. And I have, in my own little ways, but I can do more. For way too long I've sat around complaining about certain things that can only be fixed at the town council level, and it's time for me to put up or shut up."

Her mouth twisted into a self-conscious smile. "If you haven't figured out by now, I'm not one to shut up, so…"

"So, you're the bimbo running for mayor."

She laughed. "Yeah, that's me. I like to think Grandma wouldn't put it quite that way."

"I'm sure she'd be proud of you."

Ginny glowed. "Just for that, I'm going to give you

dinner." She leaned in and kissed his cheek, and the pure affection in the gesture caught him by surprise. His body's reaction was significantly less surprising, but before he could catch her around the waist and pull her down on top of him, she bounced off the sofa. "Come on into the kitchen. Everything's ready."

Before dinner went on the table, he had some cards to put there first. He stood and snagged a couple fingers into the back pocket of her jeans, stopping her in mid-stride. She turned to him and raised an eyebrow.

"I may not be pursuing many at the moment, but I know what goals are. I understand why running for mayor is important to you. I realize this"—he pointed to both of them—"is complicated, and risky, and a really bad idea, but we both know it's going to keep happening. For some reason, right now, we both need this in our lives. I can't explain why, but I can tell you one thing. Uncle Sam trusted me with all kinds of delicate situations, and you can, too. I know how to be discreet. I'm trained for stealth." Time for the hard sell, because this mattered. Apparently he did have a goal, after all. "I can get you off like a personal toy all night, every night, and nobody in town will be the wiser."

Big green eyes found his and held. "I'm counting on it."

Chapter Eleven

Do I snore? Hog the covers? What?

Ginny scowled at the useless questions circling around in her head as she followed Melody out of the pew and into the line of congregants waiting to file past Reverend Carlson. He stood at the open doorway of Bluelick Baptist, wishing his flock a final farewell as they exited into the sunny Sunday morning.

"I can't believe you were late for church," Melody muttered. "Shameful."

Ginny silently agreed, especially since she had no excuse for lingering in bed this morning, considering she'd woken up alone. Again. For the last week Shaun had shown up on her doorstep after sundown, sometimes with dinner in hand, sometimes just a hungry look in his eyes, and proceeded to rock her world in whatever way he saw fit.

She liked to think she gave as good as she got, and she certainly hadn't heard any complaints out of him, but she hadn't inspired him to spend the night either. The fact that she wanted him to aggravated her all the more, and explained why she'd feigned sleep last night when he'd slid out of her bed and dressed in the dark. It had been on the tip of her tongue to call him out on his disappearing act, but then he'd leaned down and brushed a whisper-soft, unbearably tender kiss on her forehead, and she'd kept her eyes shut and let him have his easy exit before she said something stupid like, "Don't go."

Because he needed to go, dang it. How could she convince the entire town it was time to get out from under Buchanan's political agenda if people discovered she couldn't get out from under her opponent's oldest son?

"Tom was on time." Melody nodded to the exit, where Tom stood between Justin and Brandi, shaking hands with Reverend Carlson. Ginny automatically searched for Shaun, even though she knew better. If he'd decided to take in the service, she'd have sensed his dark eyes on her from the back of the church, but he wasn't the type to loiter on the front steps, chatting with the reverend. Unlike Tom.

"Bet he's got a pocketful of talking points, too," she muttered.

"That's a safe bet," Melody agreed. "Are you ready for a church-front debate?"

"Of course. I'll be the embodiment of tact and diplomacy." She winked at her friend, but said a silent prayer as she approached the exit.

Reverend Carlson smiled at her and took her hand. "Ah, here she is—our other candidate for mayor."

At least he hadn't said, "Speak of the devil." She returned his smile, and expanded it to include Tom, who smiled back like a shark, and Brandi, who was absorbed in touching up her makeup, and Justin, who stared at her as if he could see through her clothes. Joy.

A cluster of the faithful gathered around, because hey, everybody loved a show.

"I enjoyed the sermon, reverend. It really spoke to me, especially your observation that the church, like society as a whole, thrives on new ideas, and should strive not to become entrenched in the status quo." Of course he'd said it in the context of helping the stodgy, old ways-and-means commit-tee figure out how to raise funds for new hymnals, because nobody needed another all-you-can-eat pancake breakfast or spaghetti dinner, but still.

"Really, Ginny." Tom's smile widened to the point she could count his teeth. "The reverend's sermon covered many themes. I think his underlying message had something to do with the importance of supporting our leaders—the ones with the education and experience to vet ideas and execute on the ones with merit. A lesson with broader application, don't you agree?"

So much for tact and diplomacy. "Gee Tom, are you sug-gesting *I* lack the education and experience to lead?"

"Why Ginny, you're putting words in my mouth, but as long as we're looking at credentials, I invite voters to consid-er whether they want to entrust the highest office in Bluelick to a hairdresser with a high school education."

"Maybe doing hair isn't rocket science, but we don't need a rocket scientist, we need someone who understands the challenges our town faces and knows how people would like those challenges addressed. Because I own and operate a customer-facing local business—one where people settle in and talk for a spell—I listen to people's opinions, worries, and issues all day long. I hear what's working and what needs fixing. I know what's important to the community, so I consider my job an asset."

A few murmurs of approval came from the small crowd surrounding them. She spotted Mrs. Carter, her high school English teacher, standing to one side, nodding encouragingly. "As far as my education, I graduated with honors from the Bluelick public school system. If our schools aren't good enough to produce our leaders, then I suggest the experienced, established politicians have some explaining to do, for letting our community settle for sub-par educational institutions."

Her comment—okay, accusation—generated applause, and Tom actually looked a bit flustered. "I'm not suggesting our school system is sub-par. My son goes there, for God's sake." He pointed at Justin. "But politics can be very nuanced, and complicated. Someone with more extensive education is better positioned to manage all the intricacies, and has strategic advantages when it comes to negotiating."

The reply garnered Tom some supportive comments. She didn't have a college diploma. He had her there, but… "Tell me Tom, what's your degree? The one that helps you understand all the nuances, complications, and intricacies of politics? Poli-sci? Government? Law?" Risky questions, because she had no clue how he'd answer, but when he turned red, she knew she'd hit her mark.

"Agriculture," he mumbled.

"Agriculture? Learn how to negotiate a bumper corn crop, did you?" Around them, people laughed.

"It's a very practical degree, which you might appreciate

if you had one."

His comment elicited a *point-scored* hum from the crowd, but before she could fire back, Brandi clicked her compact closed, dropped it into her handbag, and looked up. "Tommy, honey, I'm famished."

He patted her arm and flashed his game-show-host smile. "Reverend, thank you again for a thought-provoking sermon. Ginny, always so…entertaining…to talk to you."

"That went well," Melody whispered as the crowd dispersed.

"Yeah, right, if you don't count Tom getting the last word."

Melody nudged her with an elbow, and started walking down Main toward the firehouse, where they were meeting Josh for lunch. "Yes, well, he's got an agriculture degree, and he's not afraid to use it."

She laughed, despite herself, and nudged Melody back. "I don't know who won our little debate. I don't know who lost. All I know for sure is I've had my fill of Buchanans for today."

At that moment, Shaun walked out of the hardware store across the street and their eyes locked. She stared at him for one beat…two…and then forced herself to turn away.

"Liar," Melody said.

• • •

Shaun stepped from the ladder onto the roof of the cabin and watched Tyler Longfoot inspect the weathered shingles. The tall, rangy, dark-haired man Shaun remembered from a lifetime ago knelt and lifted a few loose shakes, then raised a brow at him.

"Yeah, I hate to break it to you, but you need a new roof."

He'd been up there before, so the news came as no surprise. "You're not telling me anything I don't already know. But I also know a roof is a grueling one-man project. I've ordered the materials, and I expect them Monday, along with the roll-off bin, but once I tear everything down to the boards I need to throw on the new roof pronto. So my real question is can you squeeze me in?"

Tyler squinted at the sky, adjusted his blue ball cap, and nodded. "My crew is pretty stretched, but this is a small job—smaller if you plan on helping. I can put a few guys on it later this week, assuming the weather holds."

"Sounds good." He stepped onto the ladder again. "I'll give you a deposit. Just let me know the damage."

Longfoot followed him down, descending the ladder with the ease of someone who did it routinely. Shaun flashed back to the summer between fourth and fifth grade, sneaking out of his house after dark by scaling the trellis outside his bedroom window to meet up with Roger Reynolds and some other guys in the neighborhood and explore the old Browning farm. What ten-year-old boys could resist a big, abandoned property? Some nights guys a few years older, like Longfoot and Junior Tillman, wound up there too, usually with a six pack of beer and a *Penthouse*. Good times were had by all.

"Straight labor?" Longfoot's question pulled him back to the here and now.

Shaun nodded. "Supplies are covered. I've got an in at

the hardware store." His family owned it.

Longfoot laughed, and then quoted him a fair figure.

"Done. Come in." He gestured to the door. "I'll write you a check."

He swung into the kitchen to grab his checkbook, and paused at the fridge. "Water?"

"Thanks." Longfoot accepted the bottle Shaun held out to him and ran his other hand over the newly installed soapstone countertop surrounding the matching farmhouse sink. "Nice. You do this yourself?"

"Yep." He opened his checkbook and started writing. "The slabs were a bitch to maneuver, but I got them in. I used two pieces around the sink rather than risk a break. If you look closely you can see the seams."

The other man looked closely and ran a finger down one seam, testing the smoothness. "Tight. Did you install the floor, too?"

Shaun handed him the check and then glanced down at the ebonized, wide-plank floors. "I did. I thought about refinishing the original pine floors, but they were too far gone. Too thin in the high-traffic zone."

Longfoot nodded while he folded the check and slipped it in the back pocket of his jeans. He stepped to the sink, lifted the single-lever faucet handle and let the water flow for a moment. Then he watched it drain, crouched down and looked in the cabinet under the sink. "Did your own plumbing?"

Shaun got the odd sense he was on a job interview. "I did. Here and in the downstairs bathroom."

"You picked up some interesting talents in the SEALs."

Shaun felt surprise lift his brows.

"Your father talks. He's proud."

"Well, I can't give the Navy complete credit. I participated in some building projects here and there, mostly for charity."

"What are you doing with yourself nowadays?"

Shaun pointed to the roof.

"That'll be done by the end of the week. What then?"

Good question. One he'd been asking himself whenever Tom or his mom or somebody else wasn't asking. "I'm weighing my options." Sounded better than *fuck if I know*.

"I wasn't kidding when I said my crew was busy this summer. We could use more hands, particularly skilled ones. If you're interested, let me know. I'll put you to work."

The knee-jerk refusal leaped to his tongue, because he'd been drifting and dabbling long enough. He needed to figure out his next move, not find another stop-gap, but what came out of his mouth instead was, "Thanks. I appreciate the offer—"

"One of the projects is the old Browning place."

"Oh yeah?"

Longfoot nodded. "I bought it. We're salvaging and rehabbing as much as possible. Stop by the job site next time you're down that way. I don't guarantee beer and porn these days, but I guarantee you'll take a trip down memory lane."

He never considered himself particularly nostalgic about his childhood, so the allure of the invitation surprised him. The impulse to load Virginia into the passenger seat of the Jeep and take a drive out to the Browning farm some free evening surprised him, too. He could picture her sitting beside him, a breeze ruffling her hair. A nice visual. Too bad it could never happen. In deference to her desire to keep things between them under the radar, he always came to her place after dark, parked down the street, and left well before dawn.

"What if I bring the beer and porn?"

Tyler grinned. "Then you'll be the most popular visitor we've had so far."

• • •

Something soft brushed over the bare skin along the inside of Ginny's arm. Since her wrists were tied to her bedposts, there wasn't much she could do to protect the vulnerable flesh.

"Go for a drive with me Friday evening."

Shaun's voice teased the tiny hairs in her ear canal, but the pillowcase he'd knotted around her eyes like a blindfold prevented her from seeing him. He was resourceful with the bed linens. The SEALs would be proud.

The brush swept along the underside of her breast, and then up to her nipple. She gasped as tiny bolts of pleasure ravaged her nerve endings. "What?"

The wide, soft-bristled brush trailed down the center of her torso. She writhed under the torture.

"I like this thing." He swept the brush up the same path he'd just traveled, and swirled it over her other nipple. "What's it for?"

"Applying blush," she managed, and then moaned as he feathered the mink bristles over her skin.

"I'm not even sure what that is. Tell you what, sweet Virginia, I'm going to use it to make you come." To prove his claim, he stroked down her stomach and brushed her pubic hair. She dug her heels into the mattress and raised her hips. She couldn't help herself.

"Now that's a staggering sight."

The soft fan feathered along her inner thigh. Up, up, up. She held her breath as he dabbed her most sensitive parts, and then painted her other thigh with the damp bristles.

"Please."

The brush swirled over her center again, but this time he turned it around and used the thick, wooden end. He slid it into her, but before she could say a word about the unanticipated penetration, his tongue flicked over her clit.

"Oh, God."

He rocked the handle into her, in quick, rhythmic strokes, as his mouth sucked her sanity away in long, deep pulls...sucked it right out of her body.

The brush disappeared. She had one bereft moment to cry his name before his hot, hard length filled the void. Her body clenched around him like a savior, and spiraled into ecstasy. In the midst of the chaos, he murmured something that sounded like, "Take a ride with me."

The last aftershocks of an awe-inspiring orgasm rattled through her, and she wasn't sure she heard him right. The blindfold loosened and fell away. She blinked her eyes open, and looked up at him. "Do what? When?"

He stared down at her from the distance of his braced arms, and then turned his head and placed a kiss on the inside of her left knee, and then her right. Both sat in easy range of his lips, because somewhere along the line, one of them had hitched her legs over his shoulders. He relaxed his arms and brought his body down to hers in a slow, controlled descent. "A drive. With me. Friday."

She lowered her legs and wrapped them around his waist for the sheer thrill of holding him to her a little longer, enjoying the weight of his body pressed to hers. "Where?"

"Out to the Browning farm."

Her heart kicked up a little at the invitation, inadvisable as it was. How would it look if people spotted them hanging out together? Questions would be raised, to say the least. She snuggled her face against his neck and inhaled the warm, slightly woodsy scent of his skin. "Uh-oh. Sounds like somebody's been talking to Tyler."

He untied her wrists, wrapped an arm around her, and rolled until he'd reversed their positions. "I have. We finished my roof this afternoon and I went over and checked out the site. Longfoot told me they still need hands, so I'm going to join his crew and put some work in on the restoration."

His tone remained casual, but she could tell he was excited…or at least interested. A little bubble of happiness floated up into her chest. Working with those guys would do him good. Get him out of his own head. "I'm glad you're going to lend a hand on the Browning place. Everybody in town is looking forward to seeing how the project turns out, including me. The farm is a piece of Bluelick's history, and it's been left rotting on its foundations for too long." She darted a glance at him, and then traced the letters of his tattoo. "Plus, I like thinking about you out there, all shirtless and sweaty, with Tyler and Junior and the rest of their team."

"Spend a lot of time thinking about me shirtless and sweaty, do you?"

More than she should. "Don't let it go to your head. To be honest, what I really like is the idea of you among a group of people, instead of holed up in your cabin all by yourself."

"I'm fine on my own. With a rare exception or two"— he leaned down and kissed her where her shoulder met her neck — "I prefer my own company."

"I doubt that. You went to boarding school, and then Annapolis, then the SEALs. You're used to living, training, and working as a team. You've been doing it over half your life. This wall-of-privacy thing you've got going is new for you, not the norm."

His expression told her she'd blindsided him with the insight. It shouldn't have bothered her. A lot of people discounted her as nothing more than a good-time girl and a gossip — Tom, for one — but she'd hoped she rated a bit higher with Shaun.

"Maybe I hit my limit on group participation, and now I've swung to the other end of the spectrum?"

"Nope." She forced the weight of disappointment off her chest and concentrated on him. "The fallout from your last mission and a difficult transition to civilian life shoved you to the other end of the spectrum, but you won't stay there forever. Despite what you say, part of you wants to be around people. That's why you sneak into the back of church and watch the service, or walk downtown for no reason."

He gave her a long, assessing look, and then his mouth quirked up in a small grin. "You've got me all figured out, haven't you?"

"Hardly." She nudged his foot with hers. "For instance, I can't for the life of me figure out why you want to go out to the Browning estate tomorrow evening, with me."

"Because everybody in town is looking forward to seeing how the project turns out, including you. I figured you might enjoy a preview. It's a pretty property, even with the main buildings under construction. The crew clocks out at four, so if we arrive around sunset we'll have the place to ourselves. I'll bring some sandwiches, and a blanket. We'll douse ourselves with Off, have a picnic by the pond, and watch the stars come out."

"Sounds very peaceful."

"Some of it would be," he agreed, "but you should also prepare for some vigorous moments." His big hand found her butt and squeezed playfully.

Yeah, and afterwards, he'd drop her off on her doorstep and drive home to sleep in his own bed, because God forbid he so much as nap at her place. In theory, his habit of leaving worked out for the best. The last thing she needed was Ms. Van Hendler getting an eyeful of Shaun stumbling out her door at dawn. A tidbit like that would travel down every spiraling branch of the local grapevine faster than she could say "lost credibility." But in practice, waking up to an empty bed sucked. At least it did now, for some reason.

The solution seemed simple enough to her. She could spend the night at *his* place, because the cabin offered all the privacy anybody could want. The only thing standing in her way was lack of an invitation. And that stung. It also left her conflicted about this invitation. Was this a date? Was he attempting to share something of himself with her, or let her into his life by taking her to a place he'd be spending significant amounts of time and energy? Or was he just down for some outdoor adventures?

Because she didn't know, and pride forbade her from asking, she rolled off him, stretched, and dodged the issue. "Tyler's got his hands full right now, between rehabbing the horse farm, and basically rebuilding Josh and Melody's house from the ground up after crazy Rusty Deemer burned it down."

The look Shaun sent her told her he'd noticed her retreat, but he didn't call her on it. "I heard about that. Fire-
man arsonist, right here in Bluelick."

"It's one of the reasons I'm running for mayor. The sheriff's department dragged its feet on the investigation. They
refused to take the first incidents seriously, even after Josh
told them he suspected arson. He had to force them to do
their job." She managed to refrain from adding, *And your
father did everything he could to stop Josh from pushing on
them, including threatening to fire him.*

"Don't think much of the organization, huh?"

"Maybe they do a fine job for the rest of the county, but
they treat us like the red-headed stepchild. It's not like we
demand a lot of attention and resources—normally things
around here are pretty quiet—but when we have a problem, we deserve to have them take it seriously, not just go
through the motions. A local police department would provide the support we need, at equal or better cost."

A memory niggled at her. The night Justin…er…cor-
rection, an unidentified person, had sprayed graffiti on her
wall, Shaun had been the one to insist she call the sheriffs,
and he'd been on a first-name basis with both deputies. "You
seemed familiar with the deputies who came out to take the
report. Why was that?"

He rubbed his palm over his jaw. "I almost joined the
department."

That piece of news surprised her enough to have her
sitting up and reaching for her robe. It figured. They were
already ridiculously wrong for each other. Him serving the
institution she'd made it a cornerstone of her campaign to
displace was about the only thing that could possibly make

them a more inappropriate couple. "Almost?"

"I applied shortly after I got out of the SEALs, and got an offer, contingent upon me completing training at the academy in Rochester. Your buddy Trent and I were in the same class."

And yet he wasn't a member of the department. She had a hard time imagining he washed out of the police academy. Physically, he could tackle anything. Heck, she owed life and limb to his quick instincts and reflexes. He was up to date on technology and had a solid tactical background thanks to the SEALs. Law enforcement seemed perfect for him. "So, what happened at the academy to change your mind?"

He frowned at the ceiling. "Nothing. I completed my eighteen weeks, no problem. But getting the slot was competitive, and at graduation I overheard some people talking about how I got bumped to the front of the line of candidates because Tom put in a word with the sheriff. I didn't ask him to do that, and hadn't realized he'd pulled any strings, but when I asked him, he admitted he had." He glanced over to her and shrugged. "I decided not to swear in."

Damn Tom Buchanan and his good-old-boy networking ways. Still, she figured his heart had been in the right place. He'd wanted to help his son. Misguided, sure, but understandable. "Don't let pride stand in the way of something you want. Maybe Tom opened a door for you, but you still had to walk through. You did work and complete the training. You earned the job."

"I like the way you think, but unfortunately the logic doesn't hold. At least one other applicant never got a shot at the academy because he didn't have a daddy with the juice to get him in the door. I appreciate what Tom was trying to do, and, frankly, I should have suspected something when I got the slot right off the bat—one, because I know my father, and two, because local budgets being what they are, I ought to have realized there was a waiting list of candidates I was magically leapfrogging."

"But—"

"Relax, sweet Virginia, I'm not brokenhearted over my decision." He brushed his thumb over the space between her brows, where she knew her consternation always showed. "I earned my place at Annapolis, just like the rest of my classmates. Nobody opened any doors for me. I earned my slot on my SEAL team. I earned every rank and commendation I ever received. When it comes right down to it, I'm not interested in joining an organization that operates on anything less than talent, effort, and accomplishment. The sheriff's department doesn't meet those standards." He shrugged again, folded his arm behind his head and settled back against the pillow. "It's not the place for me."

She admired his standards, but where did they leave him? "Where is the place for you?" The question came out soft, because she knew he was still figuring that out, and the answer might not involve Bluelick. A fact she'd known from the start, but let herself push to the background along with all the other reasons getting involved with him was such a bad idea.

"I don't know yet," he admitted, and she noticed the tension in his jaw and the grim set of his mouth. "I didn't think much of the way the sheriff's department operated, but the underlying work appealed to me, and, frankly, I'm good at it. Bigger law enforcement agencies are the ones hiring most regularly right now, so I submitted applications in Atlanta,

Cincinnati, and a few other places, but it could be months before I hear anything."

He looked so...remote. He'd grown up here, had family here, but in a lot of ways, this man was an island. No. Not true. An island, at least, stayed in one place. Shaun could be moving on as soon as a job offer came through. Important new fact to keep in mind, as if she needed another reason why Shaun Buchanan and Virginia Boca did not have a future.

But you have the here and now. She reached over and rested her hand on his chest. His attention immediately shifted to her. He returned the favor, slowly cupping her breast, before moving his hand down her body. Her heart raced as he closed in on one of his favorite destinations.

She wrapped her fingers around his wrist, closed her eyes, and groaned in anticipation of a Navy SEAL invasion.

His voice reached her ears a moment before the assault commenced. "I think, for the moment, I'm right where I'm needed most."

Chapter Twelve

Shaun left his Jeep in the circular driveway of his childhood home, next to Justin's Mustang, and walked into the empty hall. The silence suggested Tom and Brandi weren't around and Justin was probably bunkered in his room. Fine with him. He had a few minutes to spare before he picked Ginny up at her place, given she'd asked him not to arrive before Ms. Van Hendler left for Bingo night at the senior center. But he wasn't itching to spend them with any members of his family. That wasn't why he was here.

The cloak-and-dagger measures Ginny asked of him were beginning to chafe. He wanted to write it off as impatience with the inconvenience, but the truth tipped more toward discontent with her treating their association like some kind of back-alley booty call. Totally out of line, because she'd been upfront about her concerns from the start, and he'd signed up for this, but logic didn't change the fact that he wanted...hell...he didn't know. More. Which scared the shit out of him on a number of levels, the most obvious being he didn't have more to offer. An unemployed ex-SEAL with the wrong last name and no solid plan for his future? Yeah, that would really tempt her.

He held no illusions about what tempted her where he was concerned. Mind-blowing sex, and plenty of it. He might be drifting in a lot of areas of his life, but this was one purpose he could actually fulfill, so he'd maintain the veil of secrecy. *You don't much want to be a topic of conversation in Bluelick either*, he reminded himself. Waiting to pick her up until after her neighbor went to Bingo didn't cost them much in terms of time, and served both their goals.

The delay worked to his benefit, as it turned out, since it gave him enough time to swing by the homestead and select a beverage for their picnic. She liked white wine, and Tom had a nicer selection in his cellar than Boone's Market offered. He'd left his dad a voicemail assuring him he'd replace whatever he helped himself to on his next trip to Lexington.

He cut through the kitchen, did a quick check of the bottles chilling in the under-cabinet wine fridge and grimaced. Somebody liked lower-shelf Asti Spumanti, and he had no problem picturing Brandi sucking it down while watching TMZ or whatever passed for news in her world.

Back in the hall, he took the door to the basement. Down the stairs, past the main room with the carved, antique pool table his father had taught him to play on, an air-hockey table he didn't recognize, and a new U-shaped sectional positioned in front of a huge, wall-mounted flat-screen. A bunch of video equipment and gaming consoles blinked from a glass-fronted cabinet beneath the TV. In a far corner sat the old poker table around which Tom had hosted weekly games when Shaun was a kid.

Something suspiciously close to sadness settled in his chest. Tom had financed the perfect family room, and some no-doubt overpriced designer had brought the fantasy to life, but here it sat, dead as a tomb on a Friday night. Back in the day, Tom would have ordered pizza, his mom would have fired up the popcorn machine, and they all would have come down here to watch a movie. No way did the current version of the Buchanan family gather on the pristine, untouched sectional to talk, laugh, and play Xbox. Even sadder, if they did, he'd want no part of it.

He rolled his shoulders to shrug off the depressing thought and headed into the wine cellar. Just a fancy, temperature-controlled closet really, but along with the reds racked against the walls, it boasted a cabinet of hard stuff, and, in a small alcove behind the door, his target. A full-sized wine refrigerator.

He'd just poked his head into the fridge when the door opened behind him. He watched, undetected, as Justin strolled over to the far wall. The teenager produced a set of keys from his jeans pocket and opened the liquor cabinet.

Fucking awesome. Yes, pilfering the parental liquor was a time-honored teenager tradition, but why did it have to happen right at the moment he was pilfering the parental liquor? Shaun waited until the kid had a bottle of Johnnie Walker Black in each hand, and then stepped out from the alcove.

"Can I see some ID?"

Justin bobbled one of the bottles, lost his grip, and jumped back as it shattered on the sealed concrete floor.

"Motherfucker!" He put the other bottle on the cabinet

and turned to fume at Shaun. "You scared the shit out of me. Look what you made me do."

"It gets even worse, 'cause I'm going to make you put the other bottle back, hand over the keys, and clean up the mess."

Justin's chin came out. "Or what? You'll tell on me?"

"I'm going to tell on you anyway. The only uncertain outcome involves whether my foot goes up your ass or not. If you prefer not, then"—he held out his hand for the keys— "hand those over and find a mop."

The teenager tossed the keys on the ground and stomped off. Shaun prayed for patience, picked up the keys, and locked the cabinet. Then he turned back to the fridge and made his choice—a nice Napa Valley chardonnay. He tucked it under his arm and waited. A minute later Justin clomped back into the room, carrying a broom with a dustpan clipped on the end and a kitchen towel. He shot Shaun a nasty look, but got to work sweeping up the broken bottle. Silence, it turned out, was too much to hope for.

"You are a total, thieving hypocrite, coming down on me when you're doing the exact same thing. If you tell Dad about this, don't think I'm not going to tell him you stole his precious wine."

"Go ahead and tell him. There are two major differences between your situation and mine. First, I don't have to sneak around because Tom already knows I'm here, second—and this is crucial—I happen to be of legal drinking age."

"You happen to be an asshole," Justin muttered and dumped the broken glass into the trash bin tucked between the liquor cabinet and the wine racks. "And you drink like a pussy. White wine is for chicks."

Shaun leaned against the wine fridge, crossed his ankles and got comfortable as Justin started mopping up scotch with the towel. "Thank you, Robert Parker."

To his surprise, Justin connected the dots. "Jesus." The teen faked a shudder. "It *is* for a chick. You have a date. My mind is blown. Mr. Social is going to take a break from whatever the hell you do out there in the woods—clutch your Medal of Honor and jack off."

He laughed. Little brother definitely had a mouth on him. He could spew venom like a viper.

The kid smirked and wrung the towel out in the trash can. "First the haircut, now a date. Should have known." He went back to wiping the floor. "Who would date you?"

"None of your business."

"This can't be too hard to figure out. You don't *know* anybody. All you've done since you've been back is hang around the cabin, show up in my life at the worst possible moments, and...oh fuck...haircut." He dropped the towel and looked up. "It's the redhead, isn't it?"

Wonderful. Justin could be Sherlock-fucking-Holmes when he put his mind to it. "Hmm. Last time we discussed this—about five seconds ago—I believe I said it was none of your business. Nothing's changed."

Justin picked up the towel and gave the cement a few more swipes. "Man, Dad is going to shit a brick. She's like, enemy number one around this house. But I'd do her. She's so freaking hot, running around town in her tight little jogging shorts. You can tell she wants it, and one of these days I'm going to give that firecrotch a—hey!"

His hand found the collar of Justin's polo shirt and he hauled the kid to his feet before he fully realized what he was doing. When two wide, alarmed eyes locked on his, he transferred his grasp to the front of Justin's shirt and dragged him in until their faces were inches apart. Then he slammed him against the door and wedged his knee into Justin's balls forcefully enough that the kid turned white.

"You stay the hell away from her. Got it? You come near her, or her salon, or anything having to do with her, and you are going to be in a world of hurt. World. Of. Hurt." With each word, he increased the pressure of his knee in Justin's groin. When those wide, panicked eyes started to roll, Shaun released him.

Justin stumbled, caught himself on the liquor cabinet, and scrambled to his feet. "Get the hell off me, you pervert." He side-stepped toward the door, staying out of Shaun's reach. "Are you threatening me?"

"I'm *advising* you. If you're smart, you'll listen. Don't fool yourself into thinking you got away with something the other night, because—"

"I don't know what you're talking about."

Maybe he did, maybe he didn't. Shaun would never be able to prove anything based on one offensive word, but he could do his best to scare the kid from trying anything else. "I mean it, Justin. Don't go near her, or her salon. It won't end well for you."

"You're out of your friggin' mind. Section eight or whatever the hell they call it."

And with that brotherly parting sentiment, he slipped out the door.

• • •

Ginny adjusted her sunglasses and admired Shaun's profile while green hills divided by white wooden fences zipped past. He had the top off the Jeep and the windows down. She watched the breeze blow his hair over his forehead and made a mental note to give him a trim the next time she had her scissors handy. The warm summer evening couldn't have been more pleasant, but he seemed agitated, in his typically battened-down, utterly controlled way. A muscle ticked in his jaw, confirming her impression.

"What's wrong?"

He glanced at her, and she experienced a little flutter in her chest at the impact of him in dark, silver-rimmed aviators. Then his lips twisted into a small smile and the flutter turned into a thousand busy butterfly wings.

"What makes you think something's wrong?"

"You."

"Me?"

"Yeah, you. Your poker-faced, show-no-emotion default setting may fool other people, but even you have your tells. And I happen to be very astute."

"I have no tells." He lifted one hand from the wheel and rubbed the back of his neck.

"There's one now. Face it, I can read you like a billboard. What's bothering you?"

He dropped his hand and glanced at her again, this time over his sunglasses.

"Oooh. That's your exasperated look. This is fun. I can play all night. Or you could just tell me what's weighing on you."

He sighed. "You might have been right about Justin spray-painting your shop."

She didn't know what she'd expected him to say, but this wasn't it. "I *know* I'm right, but what makes you think so now?"

He ran down the exchange he'd had with his brother. Her first impulse was to hug him for going to the trouble to get a nice bottle of wine for her, which only highlighted how screwed up her priorities were when it came to this man, but she forced herself to focus on the pertinent information. She blew out a breath and shook her head. "I guess there's nothing worth reporting to the sheriffs? It's not like he confessed. He just happened to use the same word—circumstantial evidence."

"Not even circumstantial evidence, and nothing the sheriff's department can do anything with. But my gut says he did it. Anyway, I hope threatening to rip his balls off scared him straight, but if not…"

"If not, my handy-dandy spy cam will catch him in the act next time."

Shaun steered into the long, winding, and deeply rutted drive leading to the Browning spread. "Yeah. Next time. In the meantime, however, he might tell Tom we're involved, just to stir up trouble. I didn't confirm, nor will I, because it's nobody's damn business, but if rumors start circulating he's the most likely source."

She couldn't pretend she didn't care. She did, and she hated the idea of her personal life torpedoing her campaign. She could practically hear Tom calling her a manipulative Mata Hari, sleeping with his son in a ruthless attempt to get the inside details of his campaign. Nothing could be further from the truth, and she could use the "I refuse to dignify that with an answer" tactic without compromising her honesty.

"As long as nobody credible catches us together, it's Justin's word against mine, and his word carries very little weight around town."

Her smile felt stiff on her lips, and Shaun looked far from happy with her reply, but she shook her head. "Let's change the subject. Tonight is all ours. I refuse to let Justin ruin it."

Shaun drove between the main house and the horse stalls, both of which bore the telltale signs of construction, and parked on the far side of the barn. "I thought we could spread our blanket out by the pond. It's down that way."

She grabbed the blanket from the backseat, jumped out of the Jeep, and winked at him. "Sugar, I know my way to the pond. Been there plenty of times." Those visits had involved skinny dipping more often than not. How long had it been since she'd indulged in an illicit swim? Too long.

He raised his sunglasses to the top of his head. "Sweet Virginia, you've never been to the pond with me."

The laugh bubbled out of her before she could stop it. Lord save her from cocky men. Or maybe not, she corrected when he hefted an insulated backpack out of the backseat, rounded the car, and took her hand.

At the bottom of the hill, she spread the blanket and then crouched down to straighten the edges. Shaun put the backpack down, sat, took his sunglasses off and hung them from the neck of his T-shirt. She leaned past him to straighten the opposite edge.

"Stop fiddling. I had no idea you were so OCD."

She shook her head and continued smoothing the blanket. "I cut hair for a living. I'm very particular about my edges."

"You realize the only real purpose of this blanket is to

prevent you from getting grass stains in some personal places once I strip off that pretty red dress and do all the things I have a mind to do to you tonight?"

His words sped up her pulse, but she stood and slowly smiled at him. "You'll have to catch me first." She toed off one boot.

He remained seated, but narrowed his eyes as she kicked off the other boot. "I'm a fast runner."

She grabbed the hem of her dress and lifted it over her head. "The question you need to be asking yourself is, 'Am I a fast swimmer?'"

His eyebrows shot up. "Sweet Virginia, you think you can outswim a Navy SEAL in that little pond?"

In answer, she tossed her dress behind her. It landed in a low-hanging branch, like a haphazard red flag. Her bra soon followed, and then her panties. Then she turned and raced toward the water, feeling the heat of his gaze on her the entire time. "I think I've got a damn good head start."

Chapter Thirteen

Shaun took a moment to appreciate the view of Ginny sprinting naked into the water, and the idea of all that bare skin sleek, wet, and pressed up against his. When she'd gone out a few feet, she dove under, as fluid and graceful as a mermaid, disappeared for almost a minute, and then resurfaced in the waist-deep water and smoothed her hair back from her face. She turned to him.

Water ran down her body, dripping from her bent elbows, the tips of her high, tight breasts, and sheeted over her flat stomach. The late afternoon sun kissed her wet skin, turning her into a glistening, golden version of perfection.

"You coming, sugar, or did you forget to pack your water wings?"

He got to his feet and pulled his boots off. Jeans and briefs came next, in a tangle of fabric, and then he tugged his shirt over his head. A second later he hit the water, and was nearly to her before he realized she'd gone under again.

He opened his mouth to call her name, and the next thing he knew, took a tidal wave straight in the face.

He spat out pond water. "Sweet Virginia, you're going to pay."

Her laugh came from behind him. "Did I forget to mention I learned to swim in this pond?"

He turned and watched her do a leisurely breaststroke over to him. She stood and wrapped her arms around him. "I know all the ins and outs."

He caught her lower lip between his teeth and bit down. "I know a few ins and outs, too." Not with regard to the pond, no, but he suspected she'd appreciate his skills in the long run. She pressed herself against his chest. Or maybe in the short run.

"You think you could teach me some?"

"I'm certain," he replied. "But you'd have to get into position."

"How's this?" She wrapped her legs around his waist.

"Getting there." He gripped her ass and waded a little deeper. "I think you're ready for your first lesson." Then, without warning, he dunked them both under the water.

She came up sputtering.

"Learn anything?"

She wiped the water out of her eyes, drew her arm back to splash him, and then froze. "Someone's coming."

"Yeah, right. Nice try, but I'm not so easily distracted."

"I'm serious." This time the panic in her voice couldn't be missed. "Crap. Crap. Crap. I think it's Junior. If he sees us, he'll tell everyone. LouAnn can keep a secret, but once Junior gets to drinking, he's a loose cannon."

Shaun turned, and, sure enough, through the trees spotted

Junior's red F150 pulling up behind his jeep. As he watched, Junior climbed down from the cab. The solid thud of a car door closing followed. "Just…hide behind me. I'll get rid of him."

She splashed past him, scrambling toward the bank. "My clothes…he'll see—"

He hooked her arm and pulled her back into the water. "I'll put them under the blanket. Stay here."

But by the time he retrieved her clothes from the branch, he was about halfway between the picnic blanket and the pond, with Junior closing in fast. There was no way he'd make it to the blanket and back to the water in time to shield Ginny.

"Hey Shaun, that you, buddy?"

Shit. He bundled her clothes up like a football and ran into the water. As he splashed to waist-deep, he scanned the pond for Ginny, who was suddenly gone. Behind him, the sound of footfalls grew louder and then came to a stop. He shoved Ginny's clothes under the water, caught them between his knees, and turned to face Junior.

"Hey, Junior. What's up?"

"Oh, you know, I left my toolbox here this afternoon, and I promised LouAnn I'd finish her fancy closet installation tonight. Since I ain't likely to get any sort of *appreciation* from her 'til it's done, I dragged my ass back here to pick up the damn tools. How 'bout you? Come 'round to cool off?"

"Yeah." Where the hell was Ginny? How long could she hold her breath? "I was driving by, and decided a swim sounded good, so I stopped…"

Junior's eyes swept over the picnic blanket Ginny had

so carefully arranged, and the thermal backpack with the bottle of white wine sticking out the top. His gaze swung back to Shaun. "Spur-of-the-moment, huh?"

"I hit Boone's for supplies first. In case I got hungry after my swim."

"Looks real, uh, romantic, with the blanket and wine."

"I thought it might be nice to"—he winced and forced the words out—"pamper myself."

"Well, I don't know about that, but I'll tell you one thing for sure. I'm tired and sweaty from hauling my sorry self out here, and a swim sounds like just the ticket." Junior grinned and reached for his work boot. "LouAnn will never know I took a ten-minute break."

Fingernails dug into his ass at the exact moment he said, "No!" The word came out more forceful than he intended. At least he knew where Ginny was now.

The shorter man straightened. "Why not, man? It's muggy as hell today. That water's gotta feel good."

"I...I'm..." Fuck it. "I'm shy."

"Dude, were you not in the military for the last ten years?"

"I was, and I never had any privacy. It scars a guy." Just like fingernails using his ass-cheek as a squeeze toy. "I vowed to myself, when I got out, I'd have privacy I'd never gotten while serving my country." He'd play the patriot card. He'd play whatever card it took to move Junior along.

"Oh-kaaaay." Junior held his hands up and rolled his eyes skyward. "I wouldn't want to get in the way of someone's personal vow, or...self-pampering...or whatever. But a guy who values his privacy as much as you do probably ought to find himself a swimming hole on his own property." With that, he turned and started up the slope.

From directly behind him, Shaun felt the water shift and heard Ginny gasp in a breath. He drew in one of his own, to cover. "Whew. Thanks man. I'm relieved you understand."

"I understand," Junior called, and continued trudging up the hill. He muttered something else Shaun didn't hear clearly, but sounded like, "I understand you're crazier than a shithouse squirrel…which still makes you the sanest Buchanan."

Ginny sat in the passenger seat, in her soaking wet clothes, staring out the window. She kept her arms crossed tightly in front of her chest, and her mouth firmly closed, but he could sense her silently stewing from a hundred miles away.

He steered the Jeep along Haybarrel Road, taking the back way to her neighborhood. "I'm sorry about your clothes."

"It's not your fault," she snapped. "You did what you had to do."

"And yet you seem a little pissed off. Just a little," he added, and held his thumb and index finger an inch apart when her eyes cut into him like twin green lasers.

"I'm pissed at myself. This was a dumb idea. I knew it. I never should have agreed to it, but I did, because I was so desperate to…" She snapped her lips closed and stared out the window again.

"To what?" He asked the question gently, while something moronically close to hope rose in his chest.

She shifted around until she faced him. He felt the weight of her gaze on his profile. "I was desperate to spend more time with you. So I did something stupid and reckless, and endangered an important goal—"

"I wanted to spend more time with you, too. I want more than a handful of stolen hours every night, after Mr. Cranston walks his dog and before Ms. Van Hendler wakes up in the morning."

The confession earned him an exasperated look. "Well great. We both want the same thing. But you've known from day one we have to keep this thing between us under wraps, so instead of driving out to a place where anybody could happen along and see us, why don't you just... Screw it. Never mind." She re-folded her arms across her chest. "If I have to ask, then you clearly don't want it to happen."

How did *he* become the bad guy? Her feelings were hurt? Did she have any idea how much it hurt knowing she'd rather pass out from oxygen deprivation and drown than stand up and admit she was sleeping with him? "What don't I want to happen?"

"Oh, come on Shaun. It's so obvious. You live in the middle of nowhere. You have no neighbors. Unlike at my house, nobody would see *me* coming or going from your place. We could spend the entire night together, and we wouldn't have to resort to a covert operation to make it happen." She sighed and turned away. "Clearly, you don't want me there."

The accusation surprised him so much he pulled over. They'd covered this weeks ago. "That's not true. You know why I come to you. I told you about my sleep problems. Under the circumstances, having an overnight guest is a bad idea."

"You're afraid my company will keep you awake? I promise I'll be quiet as a mouse."

He shook his head, to clear it rather than to disagree. "No. It's got nothing to do with you. Virginia…I'm not in control of myself when I sleep. You got a taste of it the night you cut my hair. I have nightmares. Sometimes I sleepwalk. I'd just as soon avoid scaring the shit out of you again, or worse, putting a mark on you. I don't want to accidentally hurt you again."

Her hand shot out and she landed a punch squarely in the center of his chest. Apparently she had no similar compunction about leaving marks on him, accidentally or otherwise. "Spare me the guilt and those so-called protective instincts. You didn't hurt me, you moron. I startled you, you reacted, and then I woke you up. You should be begging me to spend the night. You could finally get some rest without worrying about the consequences. I'd have your back."

"I had you pressed up against a wall, and I didn't know what the fuck I was doing."

"In case you haven't noticed, I have two good lungs, and am fully capable of speaking up. It's all about intent, in my book, and I know you'd never hurt me. I trust you. You need to trust me."

He scrubbed his palms over his face. "I don't trust myself."

"How many bad dreams have you had since the night in my salon?"

His heart pounded against his ribs. "None."

"How many times have you sleepwalked?"

"None."

"Shaun, it's time to trust yourself."

Okay. Fine. This was what she wanted? Damn him, he'd try and give it to her, and if he did inadvertently hurt her, he'd never forgive himself. He reached out and took her hand. "Come to my place tomorrow. Spend the night."

"I can't tomorrow." She pulled her hand away, raised her chin, and looked down her straight little nose at him. "I have Josh and Melody's engagement party tomorrow night, after the debate at the senior center."

That's what he got for assuming she'd jump at his invitation. He'd hurt her feelings, even if his reasons were noble, and now she was going to play hard-to-get. "Come afterwards. I don't care if it's late. I want to see you."

Her mouth softened into the slightest of smiles. She reached out and fiddled with the front of his hair. "Only if you really want me to."

He saw all kinds of uncertainty in her eyes, but absolutely no fear. "Sweet Virginia, I really want you to."

Chapter Fourteen

Ginny shifted in her seat. Surely she wasn't the only one suffering from the butt-numbingly uncomfortable folding chairs the senior center had broken out for this afternoon's debate?

Ms. Van Hendler, the moderator of the only official mayoral debate, presided over a packed house of spectators—mostly seniors—all of whom seemed perfectly comfortable. Ginny stacked her hands on the cool surface of the narrow, rectangular folding table and glanced down at her opponent seated at the other end. Tom spoke to the crowd, sidestepping a question about city taxes. He'd drawn first response, so she did her best to put her head in the game and listen to his reply. Instead she thought about the rest of her Saturday. Melody and Josh's engagement party. She'd spend a couple hours at Rawley's celebrating the happy couple. Maybe sneak out a little early and meet up with Shaun…

A smattering of applause warned Ginny that Tom had reached the end of his long-winded, time-defying, and ultimately unresponsive response. Ms. Van Hendler spoke into her microphone.

"Your rebuttal, Miss Boca?"

She cleared her throat and looked out at the crowd. "Thank you. I'm a small business owner, so the subject of taxes is near and dear to my heart…and my wallet. That said, I know my money supports many programs and services important to Bluelick. The fire department is a perfect example. Through our tax dollars, we've invested in top-notch personnel and the equipment they need to do their job safely and efficiently, and they, in return, protect our community and operate consistently within budget. The town benefits from having dedicated, local firefighters responding to emergencies, and the results absolutely justify the cost."

"Why, thank you, Ginny," Tom spoke into his microphone, all confidence. "I hired our new fire chief and spearheaded the effort to have the city council approve the funds for new equipment. I consider those successes two of the biggest achievements of my current term as mayor."

"I do too, Tom," she shot back, because she refused to appear ungracious. "But I wish we got the same bang for our buck from the county sheriff's department." She saw his smile slip and turned her attention to the audience. "Our contract with the county costs almost triple what it costs other towns our size to establish and maintain a small, local police department. We pay on par with what the bigger cities in this county pay, and yet we require fewer resources and worse, we get a much lower level of service."

Murmurs of agreement hummed through the crowd. "If I'm elected mayor, I'll propose to the city council that we establish a Bluelick police department. We have a successful local fire department and there's absolutely no reason we couldn't duplicate the success with a local police department. Doing so would reduce the tax burden while improving the safety and security of our town."

The rules of the debate didn't call for a rebuttal, but Tom spoke over the audience's applause. "Miss Boca oversimplifies a complex issue. Comparing the cost of the fire department to the cost of the county sheriff is not an apples-to-apples comparison. Our contract with the sheriff's department includes 911 dispatch, and—"

"Mr. Buchanan," Ms. Van Hendler cut him off, and held up a hand for silence, but Ginny dove into the lull.

"No. You're wrong. 911 services are provided by the county, but it's separate from the contract with the sheriff's department. The 911 calls to our fire department use the same service. All the contracts are available on the city website. I've read every word of them. I know what I'm talking about."

Tom shook his head and gave her a patronizing look. "These are long, complicated contracts, Ginny. You may have read them, but I don't think you understand them— and frankly, there's no reason why you would." He switched his attention to the audience. "I negotiated those deals. The city council and I spent weeks going over every clause with the law firm retained by the city—"

"This brings us to our next question," Ms. Van Hendler said into her microphone. "Tell us what qualifies you to be mayor of Bluelick. Tom, you have the floor."

"In a word? Experience," he answered, fielding the softball in the most predictable way. Ginny looked down at her hands to keep herself from making a face. "My family has always been active in Bluelick politics. I've served on the city council more times than I can count, I've held the office of mayor twice before, and I'm currently closing in on the end of a very successful term. Unsurprisingly, the citizens of our town have urged me to run for re-election to keep the forward momentum going. I look forward to doing so."

"And you, Ginny?"

"Sometimes people offer up the word 'experienced' when what they really mean is 'entrenched', as in, 'resistant to movement and change'. I'm not entrenched. I'm not loyal to an arrangement simply because it's what we've always done, or because I had a hand in negotiating the deal. All I ask myself is, does it work? When it comes to the sheriff's contract, the answer is no. I'm proposing a better, more cost effective solution—"

"You have no experience—"

"I know how to read. I know when this city is paying too much and not getting its money's worth." Out of the corner of her eye, she saw Shaun slip into the senior center and stand along the back wall, near the door.

Tom went on as if she hadn't spoken. "You're young. Single. You're bored with warming a barstool at Rawley's and you've decided running for mayor is the way to bring some excitement to your life. But the people of Bluelick expect and deserve more from their leaders than to serve as a momentary distraction from"—he put on a show of searching for a more polite term to use than sleeping around—"a social life lacking in long-term prospects."

What? She straightened in her chair, numb butt be damned. The part of her accustomed to saying exactly what she thought wanted to shout, "My social life is nowhere near lacking in prospects. In fact, thanks to your son standing back there, I've got all the prospects I can handle." But she couldn't very well announce to the entire audience that she'd been spending her time with Shaun. She opted to turn the focus to her opponent instead.

"Tom Buchanan, are you seriously going to challenge my moral character or my ability to keep a commitment? How many times have I stood before church and state and taken vows I ultimately failed to keep? That would be none. You've done it…let's see" — she made a show of counting on her fingers, because he wasn't the only one who knew how to draw out a nasty implication — "twice now, if I'm counting right. As far as distracting personal lives, I can't think of a bigger distraction from the duties of office than extricating myself from a seventeen-year marriage after my wife discovered I was cheating on her with a cocktail waitress young enough to be my daughter."

Someone called out, "True dat," and the room dissolved into laughter.

An angry red flush stained Tom's cheeks. "My personal life has never interfered with my duties. My path to true love has been bumpy at times, but I've never been ashamed of the company I kept. Unlike my opponent, I'm an open book."

An invisible band tightened across her chest. He knew about her and Shaun — or he suspected based on whatever innuendos Justin had provided. He wouldn't dare call her out on it. Not here. "I've got nothing to be ashamed of." It was perhaps a cautious reply, but technically true. Too bad she didn't succeed in keeping her eyes from straying to Shaun. He still stood at the back of the room, arms crossed, his attention locked on her.

"Really? Well, then, since you've seen fit to drag my personal life into this debate, and you're not ashamed of your own, why not tell everyone who you've been spending time with lately?"

"You're the one who introduced the topic of personal lives, Tom, not me." The room grew restless. Yes, she was evading the question, and no, he wasn't going to let her get away with it.

"I understand you're involved with someone...how should I put it?" He absently tapped his chin. "Someone very close to home?"

The room went pin-drop silent, and every eye in the place swung to her. Her heartbeat stopped, and then kicked in again with a slow, heavy thud. "I-I refuse to dignify such a ridiculously inappropriate question with an answer."

"Goodness, that's all our time," Ms. Van Hendler said into her microphone. "Please join me in thanking our candidates for an informative and impassioned debate!"

The audience applauded. Ginny got to her feet and risked a glance to the back of the room, but found only an empty space where Shaun had been standing. Quickly, she scanned the room, hoping he'd simply shifted positions, but before she could locate him, Tom was in her face to offer a perfunctory handshake. After that, she fielded questions and congratulations from a number of attendees.

Ms. Van Hendler bustled over—as much as an eighty-something woman with brittle bones could bustle—and handed her a bottle of water. "That was the best debate I've seen since Nixon sweated all over Kennedy in 1960. To think, when I booked you and Tom for today, all these old fogies complained about interrupting afternoon Bridge for a boring political dog-and-pony show, but when Tom called you a round-heel, and you fired back with what a faithless hound dog he is, believe me, not a soul in this room wished they'd spent the afternoon bidding on tricks."

Now she didn't have to wonder how the highlights of the debate would be recounted on the local grapevine. "Well, you know, I don't think I used those exact words…"

"No, you were very civilized, but you got your point across nonetheless. A fair point considering he went there first, criticizing your personal life. Well played, Virginia dear."

"Thank you, Ms. V." *What the heck is a round-heel?* She took a gulp of water as possibilities—none of them flattering—floated through her mind. She could almost hear Grandma saying, "Her heels are so round, any man gives her the least little push and she ends up flat on her back."

"Speaking of your personal life, have you got a new beau?"

She swallowed and exhaled at the same time, and nearly sprayed water out her nose. "What? Good Lord, Ms. V, you can't believe the desperate accusations of a man like Tom."

"Oh, I know that dear. But I believe my own eyes. I usually get up at least once a night to let Rocky in or out." She shrugged. "The cat refuses to give up his nocturnal ways. Just lately I've noticed a car parked at the end of the street. Now, my vision isn't what it used to be, especially in the dark, so I don't recognize the vehicle from my distance, and it's always gone by morning, but I started wondering if you had a new boyfriend. And then I thought about the strapping young man I met a while back at your salon. Heaven knows, when I was your age, I wouldn't have let a specimen like him pass my way without trying for...how do you young people phrase it these days? A booty call?"

Ms. V blinked up at her from behind her bifocals. In Ginny's imagination a pair of night-vision goggles replaced the glasses, and she got the uncomfortable feeling Ms. V knew exactly what was going on. Since that put the older woman at least one step ahead of *her*, she decided to take refuge in deflection. "Ms. V, I hear in your day you left a trail of broken hearts wherever you went."

"I had my fun. I won't deny. But I'm more curious about your fun, at the moment."

"I know better than to try and get anything past you." She did now, at any rate. Ginny took another sip of water and wished she'd worn something other than the green, sleeve-less silk tie-neck blouse. The fabric encircling her throat suddenly seemed to be cutting off all the air to her head. She resisted the urge to loosen it, and instead scanned the crowd again in another fruitless search for Shaun.

She caught a man at the back of the room eyeing her from behind mirrored sunglasses. She didn't recognize him, but there was something familiar, and slightly disapproving, about him.

"Ms. V," she leaned close, and lowered her voice, "who's that man over there by the exit."

The older woman craned her neck to see. "Oh, my. How interesting."

"Why? What's so interesting?"

"That's Jim Bob Butler, the county sheriff."

• • •

"How late do you think you'll stay at the engagement party?"

Shaun's question flowed over the Escape's speakers as Ginny pulled into Rawley's parking lot. "No later than ten. Three hours is plenty of time to congratulate Melody and Josh."

"Just so we're clear, that was me determining how soon I can expect to have you naked, wrists tied to my headboard, panting my name."

The image he described caused a hormone cascade so powerful her knees went weak, and she thanked God she was already sitting down. "Sooner than you imagine if you keep being so clear," she said, and cut the engine. "Though I'm not really a tie-me-to-the-headboard kind of girl."

"You prefer I bend you over my footboard instead? Sweet Virginia, that's no problem."

"No. Well, maybe… It's just I've been told I'm pretty good with my hands. Seems a shame to tie them up." He laughed and a little of the anxiety she'd been carrying around since the debate lightened. "You're not upset about the…um…the debate?"

"We should talk about it. Later."

Uh-oh. The tone of his voice didn't change, but the words struck her as slightly ominous. "You warned me Justin might tell Tom, but I didn't think Tom would take aim at me like that at the end of the debate. I dodged the bullet—barely—but I should have planned a better response."

"Better than a lie, you mean?"

Now she heard a note of censure, loud and clear. "I didn't lie," she replied, knowing she sounded defensive. "It was more of a 'no comment'. What did you want me to say?"

"Uh-uh. I'm not going to put words in your mouth. I've

got other plans for it."

Okay, that got her cascading again, but she took the phone off speaker, even though her windows were closed, and replied, "We have to be more careful from here on out. Ms. Van Hendler cornered me after the debate, mentioned seeing a car she didn't recognize parked on our street, and asked who I've been entertaining these past few weeks. She didn't come right out and say it, because she can play cat-and-mouse like a damn panther, but she suspects it's you, especially after what Tom said." She took a deep breath before continuing. "It's like the walls are closing in." To combat the feeling, she opened her door a few inches.

"We are being more careful," he pointed out. "Any more careful, and I'll have to drag my ass back to Annapolis for the latest covert training. This need for secrecy disappears after the election, right?"

"Yes." *Unless I win.* Obviously, if she became mayor the secrecy would have to continue. She couldn't risk her reputation, or hamstring her effectiveness as a leader by getting caught in a sex scandal, which is exactly what sleeping with her adversary's son would amount to around these parts. Something told her not to bring that up right now. They were already balanced on a tightrope over what felt like a huge, gaping argument. Shaun sounded annoyed with the precautions—she refused to call it deceit—they were taking to avoid discovery. Tonight wasn't the time to talk long-term strategies. It might not be a conversation he was willing to have—ever.

The realization hurt more than she expected. "The election will definitely change things," she murmured.

"Good. So we'll be careful a little bit longer. Hopefully

our luck will hold out."

Her interior light cast a glow on the strip of pavement visible beneath her door. A new penny shined up at her. She leaned down, retrieved it, and held the tiny talisman in the center of her palm. The profile of honest Abe faced up. "Speaking of luck, I just found a penny."

"Great. Bring it with you tonight."

"Why?" She tossed it into the cup holder in her center console.

"Heads, I tie you to the headboard. Tails, I bend you over the footboard."

"Oh." *See? There you go. He's all about the sex. This will fizzle out sooner rather than later. He'll move on as soon as a job comes through.* The thought should have leveled her out, but instead her misguided heart bashed into an iceberg of disappointment and started sinking into her stomach.

"It's only fair you make the toss," he said. "I've already gotten my wish."

"Have you?"

"I get to fall asleep with you in my arms, and wake up to the prettiest green eyes I've ever seen."

Life boats launched. Heart rescued. Still, she couldn't help stating the truth. "I browbeat you into it."

"Virginia, I think you know me well enough to know I wouldn't have asked if I didn't want you here. But since you appreciate clarity, let me be clear. I want you. In my bed. Tonight. Don't be late."

"Or what? You'll start without me?"

"I'll start when you get here, but you can forget about choices like headboards or footboards because you won't make it past the hood of your car."

Next thing she heard was a dial tone. She hit disconnect, slipped her phone into her purse, and stared out the windshield at the hood of her car. The height and angle offered a thousand fascinating possibilities, and she wondered what constituted "late". What if she started the engine and drove to his place right now? It was well after ten o'clock… somewhere.

A knock on her driver's side window startled her out of her panty-melting musings. She turned to see Ellie standing on the other side, Tyler just behind her. Lifting her bag onto her shoulder, she exited her car. "What up, party people?"

"Your polls, from what I hear," Tyler drawled, and led the way to the pub. "Ellie says you kicked ass at the debate this afternoon."

"I said you kicked butt."

"Well, thanks, either way. I felt like it went well."

"Sorry I missed it." He held the door open for her and Ellie.

They passed through and stepped into the crowded bar. "That's okay. I know you were working. And you're doing good work. Melody's over the moon about the plans for the cottage."

"We aim to please… Hey Junior."

Junior closed in on them, a couple of longnecks dangling between the fingers of his right hand and a glass of white wine in each fist. Voice like a bullhorn even in the crowded bar, he boomed, "Hey Ty, Ellie." He passed Tyler a beer, gave Ellie a wine, and then turned to her. "Red, LouAnn told me you handed Tom Buchanan his ass in his hat today at the senior center." He passed her the other wine and tapped his beer against the rim of her glass. "I salute you."

Around them, other patrons turned their way, lifted glasses and cheered their agreement.

"Thanks Junior. Thank you, everyone. Remember to vote on Tuesday."

The reminder garnered her a halfhearted response, which told her apathy might be her real opponent, because Tom's cronies would be the first ones in line at the voting booth come election day. But she didn't intend to turn Melody and Josh's engagement party into a political rally, so she let it go.

"Where's LouAnn?"

"Aw, she's around, just avoiding me," Junior replied. "Double D's pissed because I didn't go with her to the debate this afternoon, even though she knows damn well we had a fuckload of antique barn wood coming in today at the Browning site."

"The place is really coming along. I was out there yesterday evening and I could almost visualize the end result."

"That so?" His eyebrows nearly disappeared under the rim of his backward-facing ball cap. "Who gave you the tour?"

Holy crap. Not a drink in her and already she'd put herself in a compromising position. She couldn't stand in the middle of Rawley's and respond, *Shaun Buchanan. You almost caught us skinny dipping.*

"No tour. I was out that way just…because." *Smooth.* "I got a glimpse at some of the progress, from a distance. Oh, look, there's LouAnn, standing by Melody and Josh. I'm going to pop over and say hi to them."

"Tell LouAnn to let me out of the dang doghouse. If she knows you're not holding a grudge against me for missing the debate, maybe she won't either."

"Don't worry." She patted Junior's burly forearm. "I'll smooth things over for you." With that assurance, she winked to the rest of the group and made what she considered a very narrow escape from the trap her big mouth had nearly landed her in. What the hell was wrong with her?

You're not used to keeping secrets. You've always been free to talk about whatever's top of mind. And Shaun occupied the top slot more often than not these days. Not because he should have been off-limits, or because being with him put one of her most important goals in serious jeopardy, or even because he completely owned her body with barely a touch. Shaun occupied her thoughts so pervasively because he was…Shaun. A cocky, controlled, tortured, sweet, complicated, aggravating man—and if she didn't watch herself…

Right. Something to keep in mind while trying not to accidentally out herself to the entire bar as one half of the most scandalous couple since members of the flock caught Pastor "Fire and Brimstone" Johnson giving his own personal brand of communion in the rectory with a Russian mail-order bride.

Three hours later, as she said her good-byes and walked to her car, she gave herself a mental high-five for succeeding—at least in part. She'd nursed her single glass of wine all night, congratulated the happy couple, spoken to almost everyone at the pub, and managed to keep her lips zipped about her personal life. But despite the triumph, the evening planted a seed of something restless inside her—or maybe the seed had always been there, dormant, waiting for optimal conditions to take root and grow. Conditions like watching Josh and Melody cuddling, whispering and glowing with happiness all night, noticing how the hand he rested casually around her waist slipped down to squeeze her butt when they thought nobody was looking. Layered on that? Tyler and Ellie. They weren't joined at the hip tonight, but his silent, obvious radar tracked Ellie no matter where she circulated, and her brown eyes always slid back to him as if she felt his gaze as palpably as a touch.

Roger Reynolds, Bluelick's golden boy—not to mention Melody's high school sweetheart and ex-fiancé—had come with Doug, a friend from law school. As she'd talked and joked with them, the real reason Roger and Melody had never worked out slowly dawned on her. *Gosh, what a waste*, she thought, looking at the two gorgeous men, but when she noticed how Doug's gray eyes zeroed in on Roger's mouth when he spoke, and how Roger's hand constantly found Doug's shoulder or arm, she realized not a damn thing was going to waste.

Hell, even LouAnn and Junior threw off sparks. He circled around her, trying to charm his way back into her good graces, not to mention her skimpy halter dress. She pretended to make him work for it, even though they definitely won tonight's unofficial vote for couple most likely to be all over each other as soon as they stepped into the parking lot.

Everyone she knew seemed to be pairing up, falling in love, and riding off into the proverbial sunset. And she was thrilled for them, really, but witnessing all the coupledom made her wish for the same.

She climbed into her car and faced facts. Love simply wasn't in the cards for her right now. There were too many other things in the way. She started the car, steered out of the parking lot, and herded her wandering thoughts into a strict line. Why couldn't she enjoy amazing, illicit sex with a man she genuinely *liked*, and leave well enough alone?

Because you're falling in love with him.

Oh, God. She was. Totally and hopelessly. Her heart lurched into her stomach. What the hell was she going to do?

You're going to turn this car around right now, because the road you're on leads straight to heartache.

A self-preserving or chicken-shit instinct kicked in. She glanced in her rearview mirror to make sure she didn't surprise anybody, and then whipped a U-turn in the middle of the empty street.

Red and blue lights immediately flooded her car and, behind her, a siren blared. Goddamnit. She drove a few more feet to where the shoulder widened enough to allow her to pull completely off the road, stopped her car, and rested her forehead against the steering wheel. First time she'd been pulled over in her entire life, and it had to happen now. Maybe the deputy—hopefully Trent—would let her off with a warning? The slam of the cruiser door had her lifting her head and reaching into her glove compartment for her registration. With her free hand, she hit the button to lower her driver's side window. The crunch of footsteps on gravel stopped by her door.

"My registration is in here somewhere," she said, without looking up. "Just give me one second."

"You've got one second to put your hands on the wheel where I can see them."

What? Her annoyance congealed into dread. She straightened, put her hands on the steering wheel, and came face-to-face with Deputy Crocker. Did he remember her?

"Show me your registration, license, and proof of insurance."

"They're in my glove compartment and purse, respectively. I need to move my hands off the wheel to get them."

"Don't get smart with me, Miz Boca."

Yep, he remembered her. "Just giving you fair warning." She released the wheel and dug into her purse for her license and insurance card, pleased her hands remained steady and her voice sounded calm. Hopefully Crocker couldn't tell her heart was trying to pound its way out of her ribcage and a cold line of sweat ran down her spine. She handed her license and insurance card over, and then fished the registration from the glove compartment and passed the document to Crocker as well.

"I'll be back," he warned and sauntered to his cruiser.

She faced forward and fought back shivers as she watched him through her rearview mirror. When he crammed himself into his car and got on the radio, she grabbed her jacket from under her purse and slipped it on. In the process she tipped her purse over and some of the contents spilled out onto the passenger seat. She stuffed her wallet, brush and breath mints back into the bag, picked up her cell phone to do the same, but then paused. Crocker and his "get your hands on the wheel" attitude freaked her out, and that freaked-out part of her really wanted to call Shaun and…what? Have him monitor the situation via cell phone? That made no sense. Especially since Josh, the fire chief, and Roger, a respected local attorney, were less than three hundred yards away, in Rawley's. She should call one of them to come out and make sure Crocker didn't shoot her if she scratched her nose without permission.

The slam of the cruiser door took away her options. No time for a call. Going with a rogue impulse, she hit the camera icon on her phone. It took her only a second more to toggle to video. She pressed play and dropped her phone into the pocket of her jacket. The camera wouldn't pick up anything worth viewing, but the audio…

Crocker opened her driver's side door and stared at her in a way that made her feel like a raccoon caught in a foot-hold trap. "Miz Boca, step out of the car."

Uh-oh. She did as he asked, never taking her eyes off him. "Is there a problem, Deputy?"

"Several problems. Making an illegal U-turn, reckless driving, driving while intoxicated, fleeing police…"

"What?!"

"You heard me." He turned her around so she faced her car, and brought her wrists together behind her back.

"I made a U-turn on an empty road. I didn't drive reck-lessly and I'm *not* intoxicated. Administer a field sobriety test, or, better yet, breathalyze me."

"We'll test you at the station."

Cold metal touched her wrist. Handcuffs. She blinked back tears. This could not be happening. "It will show I'm not drunk. I also didn't flee—"

"You continued driving after I flashed my lights at you." He secured the cuff around her other wrist. "I turned on my siren and gave chase."

"I'm a measly fifty yards from where you flashed your lights. I never accelerated. I pulled over at the nearest safe place." She tried to turn around, but he manhandled her back against the car.

"Tell it to the judge. Virginia Boca, you're under arrest."

Chapter Fifteen

At ten o'clock, Shaun uncorked another bottle of Chardonnay he "borrowed" from Tom's wine cellar, poured a glass
for his soon-to-arrive guest, and strolled outside to sit on
the porch steps. At ten thirty, he went inside, grabbed his
cell phone off the kitchen counter and checked the display.
No missed calls, no voicemails, no texts. By eleven, he'd left
a voicemail on Virginia's phone and then sent a text. When
eleven thirty came and went, with no response to any of his
messages, including the additional text message he sent, he
gave in to the worry gnawing at his gut, and got in the Jeep.

He knew where she wasn't—neither the camera on
her porch nor the camera at her salon had sent his phone
any alerts. Hopefully, she was still in Rawley's, talking and
laughing with her friends, completely oblivious to the time.
He could handle slipping off her radar in the midst of a big
engagement party for one of her closest friends. What he
couldn't handle was not knowing where she was. His mind

took the uncertainty and ran in too many unacceptable directions.

A drive past Rawley's, however, confirmed her car wasn't in the parking lot. He hadn't passed her on the drive in, and he still hadn't heard from her. He considered going into Rawley's and asking after her, but people didn't know him here anymore, and even those who would recognize him, like Tyler and Junior, didn't know about his relationship with Virginia—he'd come off like a stalker. Plus…a shrapnel-sharp thought detonated in his head…if she'd left with a guy, nobody inside the bar was likely to spill the information to a virtual stranger. He kept driving, and ended up at the only logical place.

Her doorstep. He parked the Jeep up the street, more annoyed than ever about the need to pretend he wasn't there to see her, and climbed her steps. And waited…and waited…and waited. Over an hour of waiting before the sound of a car engine approached, and then suddenly ceased instead of fading. Doors slammed. Footsteps advanced up her steps, and then stopped. A deep, masculine voice said something he didn't catch, and then her unmistakable, husky voice replied, "Roger, I can't thank you enough for tonight."

Okay, Roger was dead, whoever he was. Shaun got to his feet and prepared for a confrontation.

"It was my pleasure. Honestly. I'm glad I could get you off. Call me anytime."

"Don't take this the wrong way, but I hope I won't need your expertise again anytime soon. I really appreciate you coming to my rescue."

Her words sounded so heartfelt, Shaun wanted to punch the door.

"Ginny, before we call it a night, can I talk to you about something you said earlier?"

"Sure. Of course." He could picture her brushing her hair away from her face and looking up at this Roger asshole with her big, green, thankful eyes.

"The friend you had plans with tonight…before…you never mentioned a name."

"You noticed that, huh?"

"I did. You're not one to keep secrets or hold back details, so the omission stuck out to me. Is something wrong there?"

Her laugh was a monument to irony. "So much wrong, I can't even tell you. I can't tell anybody."

"Is this person important to you?"

He didn't hear her response and imagined she'd answered with a head gesture.

"Can I give you some advice—one friend to another?"

"Always."

"After Melody and I broke up I became kind of an expert at keeping an important relationship under wraps, mostly to avoid judgment from others. I justified the measures I took by telling myself my private life was nobody else's business, but eventually, I felt like I was living a lie. The lie infected all my relationships, including the one I was trying to protect. It infected my perception of myself, too, in very negative ways. I didn't respect myself anymore—didn't respect how I slunk along, hiding, as if my real feelings were something I ought to be ashamed of. You're an open person, Ginny. Always have been. I'm not saying you should take out a front page ad in the Bluelick Bugle and announce anything, but there's some grace and dignity in just living your life as you want, with whomever you want, and letting people draw their conclusions—whatever they may be. I'm really glad you called me tonight, but I can tell I was second choice. This other person is who you really wanted to call."

Okay, this guy made some excellent points, but she had called Roger, and he'd responded to the call—second choice or not. Hearing his worst suspicions confirmed made his fists clench and his stomach tighten.

"It's complicated," Virginia responded in a soft voice.

"Is he married?"

Their footsteps resumed.

"No! I would never—"

"He's got a bunch of kids?"

"No. It's nothing like that."

"This doesn't sound too complicated, if you ask me."

They rounded the shrub-lined stairway and came into sight. He stood, and the movement immediately snagged their attention. The tall, blond man stepped protectively in front of Virginia and Shaun recognized him as Roger Reynolds. His childhood friend. Her current fuck-buddy.

Surprisingly, Roger recognized him too. "Shaun Buchanan. Man, it's been years. I heard you were back in town, but…what are you doing here?"

Roger had always been a sharp guy, and he didn't take long to answer his own question. Then his eyes widened. He turned to Virginia—who was also pretty sharp, and now stood between Roger and him. "Wow. Congratulations. I believe you just became queen of complicated."

Utter silence followed the observation. Shaun fought against a tide of jealous, senseless rage rising inside him. Maybe Roger smelled it on him, or saw something in his eyes, because he cleared his throat and squared his shoulders. "Ginny, honey, would you do me a favor and get me some water?"

"That's an excellent idea," he seconded, never taking his eyes off the blond man. "Go into the house."

She crossed her arms and eyed them both. "No. And no. Either everybody checks their testosterone at the door and we go into the house together, or I stay right here and explain why you"—she poked Shaun in the chest—"owe Roger an apology."

It occurred to him, technically, he didn't have any claim to her. Yes, they'd let a one-night stand evolve into something else, but they'd never talked about exclusivity. He'd never demanded it, she'd never offered, and the fact that because of complacency, or unwillingness on his part to admit what he wanted, he actually stood squarely in the wrong tonight only intensified his frustration. "We had plans tonight. I won't apologize for expecting you to show."

"Well, that was impossible, because I got arrested."

His hands were on her before he knew he'd moved, holding her shoulders, sliding down her arms, seeking assurances she wasn't hurt. "What happened? Are you okay?"

"I'm fine," she snapped. She wrapped her arms around her waist and stepped out of his reach, but not before he caught the wounded look in her over-bright eyes. Feisty, sassy, self-assured Virginia was holding herself together by a thread, and one wrong move from him would snap it. Problem was he didn't have a right move, because leaving her alone was out of the question.

"A baseless arrest," Roger said, "in my unbiased legal opinion. She committed a minor traffic violation, and

Deputy Crocker dragged her in on everything from DUI to fleeing police. Unfortunately for him, her breathalyzer results made the DUI charge look like a joke and the distance between where she committed the traffic infraction and where she pulled over didn't support a fleeing charge. Additionally, Ginny thought to activate the video on her phone when Crocker pulled her over, and he neglected to frisk her, so she recorded the entire arrest. I simply pointed out to Sheriff Butler all the flaws in the charges, and suggested the deputy's true motive was to harass a woman known as an outspoken critic of the department. He wasn't originally sold on my take of events, but then I played the recording so he could judge for himself. I also invited him to think about how the recording might sound to, say, viewers of the local news."

He smiled and shrugged. "Butler agreed to forget tonight ever happened if we agreed to forget about the recording. After consulting with my client, we decided it would be best to let both parties put the whole, unfortunate incident behind them. I drove Ginny home, since her car is stuck in impound until tomorrow morning. And that brings us all up to date." He folded his arms, glanced down at his watch, and then added, "My God, look at the time. We should get going. Let Ginny get some rest."

"I'm staying." He didn't care how high-handed he sounded. She didn't want him in the house, fine. He'd stay on the porch. But he'd stay. He didn't miss how Roger's attention shifted to her, silently seeking confirmation. Some tightness seeped out of his muscles when she lifted and dropped her shoulder in a *suit yourself* gesture.

Roger leaned in, received a hug and kiss from his client,

paused to shake hands with Shaun, and then disappeared down the steps. Stillness descended. He was still pissed as hell, but he also wanted to wrap her in his arms and hold her, just to reassure them both she really was all right. The impulse didn't mesh well with the cold front coming off her. Virginia wasn't the silent type, though, and he doubted her ability to freeze him out forever—especially if he chipped away at her.

"Otherwise, how was the party?"

Her laugh held more sarcasm than amusement. "Otherwise, Mrs. Lincoln, how was the play?"

"Something like that, yeah."

She pulled her keys from the bottom of her handbag and unlocked the door. "The party was great." He followed her inside and waited while she dropped her keys, handbag and jacket on the small table just inside the entryway. "Josh and Melody are so happy together, which is all the sweeter because they really worked to get to where they are now— overcame a lot of personal obstacles—not to mention an arsonist."

She didn't turn to face him. He deliberated, then pulled the conversation forward. "Who'd you walk out with?"

"Nobody." With an irritated sigh, she stomped a few steps away from him. "Don't bother saying it, I already know. I walked out all by myself like a dumbass with a target on my back."

He closed the gap and ran his hand over her back, down each tense muscle under the thin, cool silk of her blouse. "I didn't say that, or think it."

"No? Well fine, maybe it was me who thought it, but not until it was too late and Crocker was in my face telling me I had one second to put my hands where he could see them."

The words came out in a rush and ended on a hitching breath. He took her shoulders to turn her around, but she shook him off.

"I'm tired, I'm sweaty, and I don't want to talk about this. What I really want to do is take a shower and wash the whole god-awful night off me."

"I'm proud of you for staying sharp even though you were frightened."

Now she turned around, eyes flashing. "I wasn't frightened, I was angry. Angry at myself for giving him an excuse to pull me over, angry at him for misusing his authority to intimidate and harass me, and furious when he ordered me out of my car, and"—her voice broke into a muffled sob and she didn't resist this time when he gathered her to him—"h-he forced me up against the vehicle and slapped cuffs on me, all the while running down a list of b-bullshit charges l-longer than my arm."

Hot tears dampened the front of his shirt. He scooped her up into his arms and carried her toward the bathroom. "He wanted to scare you."

"Well, it worked," she admitted this time, not lifting her face from his chest. "There was nobody around, and nowhere to run, and…and…nothing I could do…"

He set her on the bathroom counter, took her face in his hands and tipped her head up until their eyes met. "Shh. You did everything right," he said softly, and brushed her hair back from her tear-drenched cheeks. "You handled yourself perfectly." He punctuated the assurance with a quick, hard kiss that ended up a little more desperate than he intended. *Go slow*, he reminded himself. *Be gentle*. "But next time…" He held her face when she groaned and tried to look away. "Next time you so much as see a flashing light in your rearview mirror, the first thing you do, Virginia, is call me, understand?"

"I can't—"

He didn't let her finish, simply brought his mouth down on hers and swept the objection away with his tongue—and all his slow, gentle impulses crumbled to dust under the weight of his frustration. Spending hours simmering in his own worry before getting flash-fired by a hot blast of jealousy did nothing good for his control. "When you need someone, damn it, you call me. I'm done being your dirty little secret."

As soon as the words were out, a boulder rolled off his chest, and he almost staggered from the disorienting sense of weightlessness. He quickly reeled himself in. He might not have his shit completely together, but he had this one thing figured out. He wanted her. He was falling in love with her, and keeping their relationship under the covers wasn't an option anymore. "I'm the one. Understand?"

Slender arms locked around his head. "I need you now," she whispered and pulled him into another kiss. She was side-stepping his request—hell, demand—but her sob flowed into his mouth and tore at him. He took it. Absorbed it. Devoured it. At the same time, he pulled off her clothes until he found the flesh-and-blood woman beneath. His fingers trailed over smooth, pale skin and she shivered despite the heat.

Her energy, the power of her personality, made it easy to forget how small she really was, but tonight he took in her slim shoulders, delicate frame, and wondered at the weight she carried around so effortlessly—people's problems, including his own, expectations, including the ones she heaped on herself, a desire to bring about positive change. And for all her trouble, payback tonight had taken the form of a targeted incident designed to hurt her reputation and leave her feeling helpless and afraid. Crocker hadn't succeeded, thankfully, but her tear-streaked cheeks offered a gut-twisting indication he hadn't completely failed either.

She shivered again and wrapped her arms around herself.

He opened the shower door, turned the water on and let it run until steam filled the small, tile enclosure. "Come here." He put her under the spray, admiring how the water turned her hair to liquid fire. She sighed and unfolded like a flower bathed in sunlight. He pulled off his clothes and shouldered his way into the tiny cubicle with her, moving carefully as he backed her up against the tile wall. The sight of water running over her skin, beading at the tips of her tight, up-tilted nipples, rolling in thin rivulets down her flat stomach and into the tidy landing strip of curls between her legs sent his needs surging. He silently reminded himself his purpose tonight centered around seeing to her needs—her need to feel safe, protected and taken care of for once, instead of attending to others.

With that in mind, he poured shampoo into his palm. "Turn around."

Big, tear-bruised eyes stared up at him, confused. "You're going to shampoo my hair?"

"For starters." There wasn't a lot of room, but he managed to turn her around, and, keeping his elbows in, worked the shampoo into her hair. He moved his fingertips in slow, steady circles over her scalp. After a moment she sighed and let her head fall back.

"Feels good?"

"Mmm-hmm."

To him, too. When the lather slid down her back, his hands followed suit, massaging the long muscles on either side of her spine while the fragrant suds streamed down the gracefully curved center line. He moved his hands lower, keeping up with the lather. She shivered yet again, but this time he welcomed the reaction, because he knew it had nothing to do with fear or exhaustion, and everything to do with pleasure. He wanted to kiss his way down the same wet trail, but there was no way to manage it in the tight confines of the shower. Still, he used his hands to coax a few more shivers from her, and then brought his mouth close to her ear. "Face me."

She turned, rubbing her slick body against his in the process. Her eyes remained closed in deference to the shower's spray, her face was flushed from the steam—and his touch. Lush, pink lips parted. "I must look a sight."

"You're beautiful." And she was, even with mascara smeared under her eyes and down her cheeks. Had he ever told her so before? If not, why had he waited?

She rested her hands on his chest and made a negative sound. "I don't feel so beautiful at the moment."

He brought his hands to her face and swept his thumbs gently under her eyes, carefully wiping the makeup away. "You are, inside and out." He continued down the soft skin of her cheeks. "My mission tonight is to make sure you feel it—and I always complete my missions." He traced the curves and dip of her upper lip with his fingertip and then brushed the pad of his finger over her lower one. They parted wider—an instinctive invitation. He brought his mouth close, but didn't make contact. Her eyes opened and she stared into him while he ran his finger down her throat, along her collarbone, and then over the slope of her breast to the tight, round crest.

She sucked in a breath.

"Beautiful," he said.

She made a move to try and capture the word—or more likely cut it off. He let their lips touch, and then pinched her nipple lightly and watched her pupils go dark and wide. She moaned into his mouth.

He squeezed shampoo from her hair and then ran his sudsy palms over her throat, and her breasts, lingering there until she arched into his touch and her low, languorous moans turned fast and edgy.

Then he went lower, moving his hand in a slow circle over her stomach. She parted her legs. He dipped his fingers between her thighs, but only grazed the outer folds. Her needy groan ended with a muted thump—the back of her head connecting with the tile wall. "I need you. Please. Make me forget everything except you, and me, and this."

His cock jumped to do her bidding. "Steady," he murmured, more to himself than to her, and hauled her up until she was braced between his hips and the wall. Her heels dug into the hollows behind his knees. "You have me, Virginia— as much as you need, for as long as you need me."

The words applied to his heart and his soul, not just his body. Her round, stunned eyes told him she'd heard the deeper meaning, too, and wasn't sure whether to trust her ears. Not the reaction he would have hoped for, but fair enough, considering she hadn't asked for heart and soul from him, they'd never discussed the future, and standing in her shower, two seconds from giving her what she *had* asked for, wasn't the time to bring up the rest of his shit. He retreated to safe territory. Sex. "For once we're going to take this slow."

He lifted his chin, brought his hand to the back of her head and captured her mouth, lingering there, gliding his tongue over hers in lazy, sweeping circles, as if he could reach some truth inside her if he could just go deep enough. She speared her fingers into his hair and made demanding sounds in the back of her throat. *More.*

He refused to rush, but he could give her more. Hand under her ass, he lifted her, let go, and she dropped down on him in one smooth, fluid slide. Her long, thankful moan echoed around him and then broke off into urgent little cries as she started to move.

"I need—I need—" she pleaded around his tongue, and struggled to find her rhythm, pushing herself until her breath came out in ragged pants and her body shook with the strain of chasing the orgasm.

"Be still. I've got you. I'm going to give you what you need."

She fought a little longer, and he had to admire her stubborn streak, but moments later she sagged against him. He gripped her hips, holding her up and keeping her flush to the wall. "Don't move. Tonight I take care of you." When she finally nodded, he withdrew a few inches, circled his hips, and sank into her again.

She sighed and her head rolled against the tile. He repeated the motion, taking her a little higher, coming back a little harder each time. Within minutes she was finding ways to break the don't-move rule—pressing her arches into his calves and using the leverage to meet his thrusts, but he stayed the course, drove her up and brought her down just a beat slower than he knew she preferred.

Her mouth found his. She sucked on his tongue with renewed fervor, pleading for speed, but he kept to his pace.

Water rained down on his head. Steam clouded his eyes. She was shaking, and that was okay, because he was shaking, too. He wrapped an arm around her waist and dragged her up, up, up… Their mouths broke apart. The rest of her body clutched at him like a necessity.

"Sweet Virginia, are you ready to move?"

Her response was husky and needy and not particularly articulate, but he knew a yes when he heard one. He let go of her waist. She slammed down on him, dug her fingernails into his shoulders and surged up, and then hung there, quivering against him for one long, tense second. And then she went over. Head back, eyes closed, she cried his name…and pulled him into the eye of the storm.

He locked his legs and rode it out, somehow managing to keep them upright. When the last shudders subsided and she lay in his arms like a rag doll, he rinsed them both and then bundled her into the thick robe hanging from the hook on the bathroom door. Probably a bit much for summer, but she didn't seem to mind. Then he carried her to bed.

They lay there, her snuggled at his side, and he watched her chest rise and fall. After a few minutes he turned out the light.

"Thank you," she murmured.

"I thought you were asleep. I would have turned it off sooner if I'd known it was bothering you."

"Not the light. Thank you for...the shower. For taking care of me." She raised her head and stared at him in the dark. "For dragging my mind away from what happened tonight and giving me something else to focus on instead."

As if he could have done anything else. "Yeah. That was quite a sacrifice, but I'm a giver."

She laughed, as he'd hoped, and settled against him again. A big part of him wanted to circle back to the whole "I'm here for you as long as you want" epiphany and feel her out...or, fuck it, just tell her, "I love you, but I'm through hiding this relationship. Make a choice. Me or the mayor's race, but if being with me costs you the election, then this town doesn't deserve you." Everything else—his job, a home-base, the future—they'd figure out. But Virginia wouldn't respond well to an ultimatum, and his timing couldn't be worse, given the night she'd had and the fact that she was about to drift into some much needed sleep. He circled back to something more innocuous...something he was curious about, nothing more.

"What was the traffic violation Crocker pulled you over for?"

Her fuzzy-edged reply almost didn't reach his ears. "...Illegal U-turn."

Chapter Sixteen

Shaun got behind the wheel of his Jeep, went to start the engine, and then stopped and waited for the weight on his chest to move. A U-turn. Maybe she'd forgotten something at the pub, but even as the explanation formed in his brain he knew it didn't hold. She'd had her purse and jacket—all the essentials—when she'd arrived home. He knew the road out to his cabin was open, since he'd driven it himself. Time to face facts.

Fact one: simple explanations tended to be correct.

You want the simplest explanation? She turned around because she changed her mind about seeing you tonight.

Flawless timing on fate's part. The same evening he'd manned up to the truth that he was in love with her, she'd stared into her rearview mirror and wondered, "What the hell am I doing, driving miles out of my way to spend the night with a screwed up, rudderless, drifter who also happens to be Tom Buchanan's son?"

Fact two: if her answer had been, "Falling in love," she wouldn't have whipped the U-ball.

He rubbed his palm over his sternum, but the ache in his chest refused to budge, and for the first time in months, he had an overwhelming urge for a drink. The clock on the dash read two thirty in the morning, which ruled out the standard Kentucky cure for a jacked-up Saturday night. Unless he pulled a Justin and raided Tom's liquor cabinet. Unlike little brother, he didn't need the key to pop the lock on the cabinet. He was debating the merits of a stop at the house when a vibrating noise snagged his attention.

He picked up his cell phone from the dash, where he'd tossed it when he got in the car, and touched the screen. The icon for the security camera registered a bunch of new images. He'd retrieved some earlier alerts of him sitting on her porch before she'd arrived home. The new ones were probably from when she and Roger had arrived, and then one of him leaving a few minutes ago, but when he tapped the icon and scrolled through the images he got a surprise.

The latest images had been recorded mere seconds ago, at her shop. They revealed a black-clothed figure spray-painting "firecrotch" across the white wall in rude, red letters. The camera's night-time resolution didn't quite turn darkness into day, but only a blind person would have trouble identifying Justin's face.

Fucking idiot. Deep down, he'd hoped his warning would do the trick, which no doubt made him the bigger idiot. He started the car and drove down the hill as fast as he could without waking the neighborhood. Once he turned onto Main, he picked up speed and closed in on the salon, but even from several feet away he could see the empty sidewalk. Only the single slash of paint hinted anyone had been there recently. Luckily, he didn't need to catch Justin in the act. A picture was worth a thousand words, or, in this case, a thousand hours of community service.

Driving straight to the sheriff's department and showing them the video would save Virginia the trouble of calling them first thing in the morning when she woke up and checked her phone. Given what had gone down last night, he didn't want her interacting with them at all—at least not until after the election. Speaking of which, Justin's prank might deal a death-blow to his father's mayoral campaign. Maybe Tom would withdraw if he saw the evidence—decide to focus on solving his kid's behavioral problems instead of fighting to keep the status quo in Bluelick?

One could hope. And the hope had him heading up Riverview Road rather than out to the Double A. The house was dark when he arrived, except for a light shining from the window of his father's study. He half-expected to see a red Mustang angled in the driveway, but instead he spotted a dark sedan he recognized as Jim Bob Butler's Buick. Maybe the sheriff already knew about Justin's nocturnal artistic endeavors? Why else would he be at the house at this hour?

He couldn't answer the question with certainty, and, in his experience, uncertainty mandated caution. He parked on the street, walked across the lawn, and let himself into the house. The entryway was silent and dark, and he did nothing to alter that status. A few steps down the hall, he picked up voices coming from his father's study. The door hung half open, and through the gap he saw Butler, in plain-clothes, sitting in the guest chair, and Tom behind the desk in his robe and pajamas, looking primed for an argument.

"Butler, you assured me after tonight, Ginny Boca would be a non-issue. What the hell happened?"

"Crocker picked her up outside Rawley's just as you suggested, but there was a small flaw with your plan, Tom. A DUI arrest only sticks if the person is, in fact, driving while intoxicated. Not only was she nowhere near drunk, she recorded the incident on her cell phone, unbeknownst to Crocker. Next thing I knew I had Roger Reynolds in my office playing a recording of Crocker threatening her like some tin-badge deputy on a power trip, and I was lucky to negotiate a "let's forget about this little misunderstanding" settlement just to keep the whole cluster-fucking mess off the front page of the Bugle."

Shit. It was a night for idiots. Shaun nearly banged his head against the doorframe, but rendering himself unconscious would be taking the easy way out. Instead he hit the record button on *his* phone and stayed where he was, just outside the study door.

"Look, you brought us to this," Butler went on. "You told me you'd discredit her during the debate, and she wouldn't stand a chance of winning, but she wiped the floor with you—"

"I know what happened at the debate. I was there, thank you very much. It's done. There's no un-doing it, but I can still win this thing. I just need an advance on the appreciation fee we agreed on, so I can give some people a proper incentive to come out on election day and cast their vote my way."

Shaun's stomach churned as he watched Butler stand and pull an envelope from the back pocket of his jeans. "There's half the appreciation fee. You'll get the other half at the usual time — once the city council votes to renew the contract with the county."

Tom picked up the envelope and glanced inside. "Thanks, Jim Bob. Thank the rest of the boys for me, too. You won't be sorry—"

"No, we won't," Butler said in a hard voice. "The boys asked me to inform you if you don't win on Tuesday, they're taking that back, out of your ass if necessary."

The envelope in Tom's hand shook and his pale face stood out in stark contrast against the dark green curtains behind him. "Hey, now, I don't appreciate threats."

"What are you gonna do, Tom, complain to the sheriff?" Chortling at his own joke, Butler headed to the door.

Shaun stepped into the shadows and listened to the sound of the sheriff's footsteps fade down the hall. His leg muscles twitched with the urge to pursue, tackle the man, and make him choke on his laughter, but, frankly, the guy didn't deserve a fast, easy take-down. He deserved to twist on the line like a hooked fish, and watch while every single person in the ring of corruption turned on him on their way down, starting with Tom.

The front door opened and closed, and the house fell silent. He pulled out his phone, stopped recording, and pushed back alternating waves of disappointment and anger. A tap on the doorframe had Tom's head jerking up from counting the hundred dollar bills fanned out across the top of his desk. His cheeks turned a guilty shade of red, but he swept the bills into the envelope and smiled. "Shaun, Jesus…always good to see you, but you scared the crap out of me. How long have you been there?"

Shaun walked into the office, sat in the chair Butler had

vacated, propped his right foot on his left knee and put his phone on the edge of the desk.

"Long enough to know we need to talk." Then he hit play.

• • •

Ginny hurried toward her front door, stopping mid-stride to balance on one foot and tug the heel strap of her black and white polka-dot high-wedge espadrille more snugly into place. She'd slept a bit later than normal—no surprise after last night—and then wasted some time sulking upon realizing Shaun had stuck to his usual MO and left sometime after she'd drifted off. What had she expected? If she'd wanted him to stick around, she should have at least stayed awake long enough to issue the invitation, but then Ms. Van Hendler might have seen him leaving this morning, and, in all likelihood, he didn't fancy that any more than she did.

He'd remained amazingly neutral about the mayoral race, but she knew him well enough to know he wouldn't willingly do something to compromise her. Yes, a small, uncertain, and no-doubt unfair part of her wondered where his loyalties would lie if push ever came to shove, but when he'd looked into her eyes last night and told her she had him—as much as she needed, as long as she needed—she'd let herself hope maybe he intended to stick. She'd let herself hope maybe she wasn't the only one wishing there might be some way to forge a future, whatever happened with the mayor's race. She'd let herself hope maybe things were changing for him, too.

And then she'd woken up alone.

She mentally kicked her butt into gear and resumed walking toward the door. None of the hoping and wishing accomplished a damn thing at the moment, but between the sleeping and the sulking and having to walk to church because her car was in impound, she was going to miss the opening hymn.

Her purse sat exactly where she'd left it last night, on the entryway table. She scooped it up, and, out of habit, looked in her wallet to make sure she had her checkbook. Jesus took checks and Uncle Sam allowed the deduction. Win-win. Her cell phone woke up from all the jostling and the screen caught her eye. She hadn't checked it since she'd passed it to Roger last night through the bars of the holding cell. Now she noticed the security camera icon showed eleven alerts.

Shaun on your doorstep. You and Roger arriving last night. Shaun leaving this morning. Even though she didn't have time to spare, curiosity got the better of her. She tapped the icon and pulled up the images. And froze. The most recent images were from the store cam, not the porch cam, and clearly showed Justin spray-painting the same obscene graffiti on her salon wall.

"Son-of-a—" She dialed Shaun's number, for no good reason except she wanted to confirm he saw the same thing she saw. And, okay, she wanted to talk to him, and, spineless as it was, she wanted him to offer to be with her when she called the sheriff to report the matter. After all, last night he'd said—

"Hello Virginia."

God, he sounded like a flat tire. Worn out and depleted. Whatever happened between them, his days of getting up at two in the morning to drive home were over, she vowed.

The man needed a decent night's sleep. "Hey sugar, have you checked the security camera? Because I did, just now, and—"

"I checked. I saw. I handled it."

Something was wrong. He sounded wrong. "What do you mean it's handled? I need to call the sheriffs and show them this video."

"No you don't. Don't call. Don't drive out there. Don't go anywhere near the sheriff's department. Promise me, Virginia. What I need you to do is go on to church."

"Go to church and let Justin get away with defacing my store for the second time? What the hell, Shaun?"

He responded with a weary sigh. "I took the video over to the house last night, to show Tom, and—"

"You showed Tom? You didn't think to wake me up and show *me*, but you showed Tom? Why would you *do* that?" Her voice rose in pitch with each word, until even she cringed by the end of the question.

"I had my reasons. If you calm down long enough to let me finish, I'll explain."

Calm down? The man had betrayed her trust and now told her to calm down? How about an *I'm sorry*? A cold, hollow ache spread through her chest. "You know what? You can take your reasons and shove them where the sun doesn't shine. I don't need an explanation for something this clear. I tried really hard not to put you in any position where you had to choose between Tom and me, but, deep down, I wondered who you'd stand by if you had to take a stand. Sucker that I am I actually thought you might stand by me. Now I don't have to wonder anymore. I know exactly where your loyalties lie. So thanks for that."

"Virginia, you don't know a damn thing—"

"I know I've had my fill of Buchanans," she hurled back, and then disconnected, because a sob kept trying to claw its way out of her throat, and she'd be damned if she let his choice reduce her to tears.

A text message immediately dinged. From him. Tears blurred her vision, but she managed to read the words.

Trust me. Please. Just go to church.

Trust him? Never again. As far as the rest, it wasn't like she had any choice. She wasn't going to call the sheriff on her own. She put her purse on her shoulder, strode out the door and shut it behind her with a wood-vibrating bang.

But if Roger was at church, she planned to show him the video and ask him to hold her hand while she pressed charges. The Buchanans might be powerful, but they couldn't buy, barter, or back-scratch their way out of this.

Fifteen minutes later she scooted into the pew beside Melody and Josh, and joined in the last verse of the opening hymn, "The Joy of Forgiveness." She recognized the back of Tom's head, occupying his usual spot in the front pew, but neither Justin nor Brandi flanked him. Instead he stood between two dark-suited men she couldn't place from her vantage point. Was Justin sleeping in after his late night spent menacing society?

She cast a quick glance toward the back of the church, not really surprised to find it empty.

Reverend Carlson motioned for the congregation to be seated, and then, with an uncharacteristically solemn face, approached the pulpit and said into the microphone, "I had a different sermon planned for today, but a member of our flock needs our ear this morning. Please join with me in welcoming Tom Buchanan."

Melody glanced at her and raised her eyebrows. She shook her head, but inside, she scrambled. What was *this* about? Did Tom think he could mitigate the backlash of Justin's behavior by throwing himself on the mercy of the church?

Tom stood and walked the few steps to the podium. When he turned to face the congregation, she nearly fell out of her seat. He looked pale, haggard—like he'd aged into every one of his fifty-some years virtually overnight. Apparently she wasn't the only one who thought so, because a little wave of concern rustled through the congregation.

This has nothing to do with Justin spray-painting your shop. Somebody's in the hospital, or the morgue, or…

"Thank you, Reverend Carlson," Tom started in a voice so rough and creaky he stopped, cleared his throat, and leaned closer to the microphone. "I appreciate the opportunity to speak here this morning. It's fitting, because church is a place for confession and forgiveness. I need to do the first and hope, in time, you'll grant me the second. But first I need to, uh…" He trailed off and dragged a white handkerchief across his sweaty forehead. "I resign as Mayor of Bluelick, effective immediately, and withdraw my candidacy for re-election."

A stunned silence followed his announcement, and then a rumble of conversation swept in as people digested the news.

Melody grabbed Ginny's arm. "Did you know about

this?"

She could only manage a head shake. Tom started speaking again and she strained to hear over the din of the congregation's reaction to his news.

"I know this comes out of nowhere, and I apologize for letting you down, but the truth is, I let you down well before today. I let all of you down—my neighbors, friends...my family. I am deeply ashamed to tell you, during my tenure as mayor, I accepted payments from the sheriff in exchange for renewing their contract with the city."

This time an audible gasp arose from the pews, and Ginny let hers fly right along with everyone else's. She never admired Tom, but she never dreamed he was on the take. Did Shaun know? She replayed their phone call in her mind. Yes, he'd definitely known this morning. When had he found out? How long had he kept his father's secret?

"I want to assure you I acted alone. Nobody else in Bluelick participated in any way. Nobody knew anything about this until last night, when my son Shaun came home and caught me red-handed. It is a sad moment, as a parent, to look into your child's eyes and know you've failed as a role model and forfeited his respect. I would like to publicly thank Shaun for being an honorable man, and requiring me to do the right thing. With his help, I contacted the FBI, confessed, and pledged to cooperate with their investigation, which has already commenced. Sheriff Butler and other officers within his department have been suspended from service pending a full inquiry. To that end, I'll be accompanying federal investigators to Louisville today and...well...I probably won't be seeing you for a while."

Conversation broke out all around as people processed

the information.

"Oh my God." Melody turned to her. "I'm sitting next to the new mayor of Bluelick."

Ginny shook her head and a punch of panic pushed all the air from her lungs. "No. Uh-uh. I don't want it this way."

Josh leaned across Melody and pinned her with a serious stare. "Man up, Boca. This town needs you. Now more than ever."

Commotion in the center aisle saved her from answering. Brandi stalked toward the pulpit, shaking off a dark-suited man who tried to rein her in. "Tom, tell this man I can't go to Louisville. I have an appointment with the landscaper to-morrow morning, for that lap pool you promised me…" Her whiney tirade trailed off into an indignant squeak as the suit snagged her arm, spun her around, and marched her back the way she'd come.

Tom's voice pulled everyone's attention to the front of the church again. "I-I know my apologies can't repair the damage I've done, but I offer them anyway, and urge you not to let my shortcomings taint your view of our public servants here in Bluelick. You have a fine, dedicated city council, and a mayoral candidate with all the ethics, gumption, and good sense you could ask for in a leader. I hope you'll give her your support. Thank you."

The two men in dark suits stood as Tom descended the pulpit, flanked him, and whisked him out the door, and that's when it hit her. *Tom Buchanan is in custody.*

Shit just got real.

Chapter Seventeen

"Hey, Miss Mayor."

Ginny looked up from the small reception desk separating her waiting area from the rest of her salon and smiled at Grady Landry, hovering half in, half out of her door. "Yes councilman?"

"Got a minute?"

"Sure." She dropped her pen and gestured him to a seat in her empty waiting area. She was in-between appointments, trying to be productive, but his presence alleviated her need to stare at the minutes of last night's city council meeting—her first as mayor—and pretend to focus while her mind stubbornly fixated on Shaun.

According to Tyler, Shaun had gone to Louisville with Tom, but he'd been away for over a week now. Was he ever coming back? She'd hoped against hope to see him at her victory party last Tuesday at Rawley's, or at her expedited swearing-in ceremony last Friday morning. She'd missed him like a vital organ, picked up her phone a thousand times to call him, but never followed through. What would she say? *Sorry about your dad. Sorry I doubted you. Um…by the way, I'm in love with you.*

Of course, he hadn't contacted her either. For all she knew, he'd kissed Bluelick good-bye permanently this time. He'd never wanted to get swept up in local drama, but circumstances and his own moral compass had landed him a central role. Who would blame him if he preferred to forget the place existed? Family didn't hold him here anymore. Tom had already put the Riverview house on the market and taken an apartment in Louisville. Justin had been shuttled to his mother in Atlanta, and Ginny had declined to press charges for vandalism because she'd just as soon not have him back—even for a day in court. Nobody had seen Brandi since the infamous Sunday. Rumor had it when the Feds had spit her out she'd returned to Rabbit Hash.

"How are you holding up, Grady?" she asked as he lowered his oversized frame into a chair. The last week hadn't been easy on a lot of people in Bluelick, including the city council. Despite Tom's assertions he'd acted without the knowledge or participation of the rest of the council, current and past members had endured long, sweaty hours of questioning by the Feds. Ginny, too, had spent quality time with investigators, and walked away with her nerves stretched to the limit, even without the cold eye of suspicion on her. The story had brought out regional and local press, who'd hovered like vultures over the town for days, before finally moving on to a high school football scandal in another county.

"Hanging in," Grady said. "Are you feeling effective, having your first major proposal as mayor unanimously approved?"

They'd voted last night to establish the Bluelick Police Department and approved an initial budget. She laughed. "Under the circumstances, I'd have to say the proposal sold itself."

"Not at all. You sold it. After you left, the other council members and I had a little chat about who we might tap to be our police chief. We're not fighting a daily battle against criminal elements here, thank my maker, but we need someone with law enforcement training, who knows when to deter by presence, and when to take action, and has experience coordinating a small team. Ideally, someone local."

She winced. "The local part is the kicker. There are plenty of deputies looking to exit the sheriff's department at the moment, but rightly or wrongly, they're tainted by Butler and his bad apples. This community needs a chief of police they can trust in the role from the get-go, not someone who might earn their trust over time."

"Yep. We couldn't agree more. And we have the perfect candidate. Shaun Buchanan."

Her heart skidded to a halt, and then took off at double-time. "Shaun?"

"Sure. He convinced his own daddy to do the right thing. Didn't turn his back or look the other way. If that's not loyalty to this town and the law, I don't know what is. People respect him for how he handled the mess, and we're not the kind to punish the son for the sins of the father. He made the tough call, and he followed through. He served our country with honor, and graduated with flying colors from the academy in Rochester earlier this year. What more could we want?"

She folded her hands and propped her chin on them. "I agree, and I… I think he'd do a great job. He's got the right background. I trust his instincts and his judgment, but Grady, I don't know what his plans are. I don't even know if he's returning to Bluelick."

"He's back. Got in last night and was on the job at Longfoot's site first thing this morning."

"Oh." She swallowed that bit of news and tried to hide her disappointment. He hadn't called. Hadn't come by. "Does he plan to…stay?"

"We're thinking you might be able to shape his plans, if you speak to him about the job. Sell him on it. Make him an offer he can't refuse."

"Me?"

"You're the mayor." Grady grinned and hefted himself out of her guest chair just as Dilly Hill bounced in to get her roots touched up, and Mrs. Hill followed.

"OMG. Ginny Boca, you're the freaking mayor," Dilly gushed, and wrapped her in a hug.

"Yeah," Ginny replied, and hugged her back. "OMG."

Forty-five minutes later Dilly danced out behind her mom, eighty dollars lighter a shade blonder than her daddy was likely to appreciate, but happy. Ginny waved at them, flipped her sign from OPEN to CLOSED, and started lowering the blind over her front window.

A figure standing at the curb drew her eye. Shaun, hands tucked into the front pockets of his jeans, staring at her.

She hurried to the door, never taking her eyes off him,

but when she opened her mouth to speak, the chaos of words rushing to be freed clogged her throat. *How are you? I missed you. Why are you back? What are your plans? I'm in love with you.* Where should she start? "You could use a trim."

Nice.

His lips tightened into a faint smile. "You're the expert."

She tipped her head toward the shop. "Just so happens I have an opening in my schedule right now."

He glanced at her CLOSED sign and then back at her.

In answer, she stepped aside, held the door open, and inhaled deeply as he brushed past. His scent, the heat of his body, his proximity—the combination triggered longing so strong it almost made her dizzy. Everything inside her ached to hold onto him, but he'd rebuilt his wall of inscrutability since he'd been gone, and she couldn't tell how he'd react. "Have a seat."

He went to the chair in front of her workstation and sat. She lingered in the waiting area for a moment, thought about lowering the blinds, but left them alone. Secrets weren't her style—never had been. If somebody walked by and caught an eyeful of Shaun Buchanan getting a trim from his father's successor, so be it. Let them speculate.

She approached the chair, while memories of everything they'd done at this very workstation the first time she'd given him a haircut blew through her mind. Her hands were less than steady as she shook out a clean cape, draped it over him, and secured the Velcro at the back of his neck. Trembling hands...not the kind of trait a smart man looked for in a person about to wield scissors around his head. She inhaled slowly, and waited for calm before she leaned past him and dug a clean comb and scissors from her drawer. Her arm brushed his shoulder as she straightened, and the heat from the small contact zinged through her, leaving no molecule unscathed.

She spritzed the back of his head with water and began working the comb through. "How have you been?"

"I'm surviving. The Feds are done with me, for the time being, so that's good."

"You look good." God, did she sound like she was hitting on him? "I mean…you know…well rested."

"I am, strangely enough. I'm sleeping again." His eyes found hers in the mirror. "I have you to thank for that."

"Not really. All I did was ask a few questions and listen."

"Listening is one of your gifts, sweet Virginia. One of many."

The sound of her name on his lips caused a spike in her pulse. She didn't know how to respond to his observation, so she offered him a quick smile and concentrated on trimming a tidy line across the back of his neck.

"Guess I should call you mayor now?"

Was he teasing her? "Virginia is fine." She snipped around his ear.

"Congratulations." This time his voice held no hint of a tease.

"Thank you." God, he might as well have been a polite stranger, instead of the man with whom she'd shared more physical and emotional intimacies than she'd ever dreamed possible. She moved around to the front of the chair and focused on his bangs. After a minute, the inside of his knee brushed her thigh. Her eyes dropped to his, but those bottomless brown depths gave nothing away.

Something inside her snapped, and she dropped the scissors and comb down on her workstation with a clatter. "Why didn't you call me? Or come by yesterday when you got back into town?"

The corner of his mouth tipped up into what someone less attuned to him might have mistaken as a smile, but she knew better than to confuse the sardonic twist of his lips for a sign of amusement. "Last time we spoke, you said you'd had your fill of Buchanans."

She raised her hands, not sure if she planned to plead with him or strangle him, and ended up lowering them again. "Last time we spoke I didn't know what was going on!"

"Here's what was going on: my stepbrother had defaced your building, my father had hatched a plan to derail your campaign with a false arrest, and was attempting to keep his sinking financial ship afloat by taking bribes from the county sheriff. Under the circumstances, I can't blame you for deciding you didn't want any Buchanans in your life."

He laughed and looked out the window at Main Street. "I can't blame anyone in town for feeling that way. But that Sunday before I left for Louisville, I called Tyler to let him know I wouldn't be at work, and why, and he made me promise to come back and finish the job when I could. I gave my word, so…here I am. They're behind schedule at the moment, so I know at least a few people in town are glad to have me back."

"You idiot man." She crossed her arms over her chest to keep from putting her hands on him. "Everyone in town is glad to have you back. You're our hero, for having the strength and courage to do the right thing, even though it meant making your father turn himself in. This town respects you, and trusts you."

"That's nice to hear, but I'm more interested in what you—"

"I'm not spouting nice words, Shaun. Grady just spoke to me today, on behalf of the city council. We've voted to establish the Bluelick Police Department and they want you as the chief of police. I'm supposed to talk you into taking the job."

The information clearly came as a surprise, and she thought she saw a flash of interest in his expression. She pressed on. "It's a chance to build the department from the ground up, almost literally. You're the perfect choice. You'd be good at it."

"I am interested, but I have certain conditions."

Interested was good. Interested meant he might actually stick around, and if he stuck around, maybe she could figure out how to convince him to forgive her for not trusting him. Her heart beat a little harder at the prospect. "Name them. Anything. If it's in my power, it's yours."

"You," he said, and his hands cupped her face. "I want you—all of you—your hopes and dreams, your body and heart. I want a chance to prove you can trust me with everything."

"I do." She wrapped her fingers around his wrists and held on, trying to underscore the truth behind those two little words with her touch. "I swear I do, Shaun. I never should have doubted you. When we spoke Sunday morning, you asked me to calm down and let you explain. I didn't. I jumped to conclusions because I was scared."

His eyes darkened. He rubbed his thumb gently along her jaw. "Sweet Virginia, don't ever be scared of me."

"I was scared of *me*," she admitted, and felt the burn of tears behind her eyes. "I was terrified because I-I'd fallen in love with you. I hadn't meant to, didn't particularly want to—"

He cut her off with a kiss. Simply pulled her in, covered her mouth with his and stripped all her defenses away until she melted against him.

"I love you, too," he said against her lips, then eased back and gave her a firm look completely at odds with the tender words. "But I refuse to keep our relationship off the radar. No more sneaking around. I don't care if it causes a scandal. We take this thing out in the open. That's non-negotiable."

She wanted to shout "yes" at the top of her lungs. From the rooftop. From the bell tower at Bluelick Baptist, but a movement outside her shop window snagged her attention. She turned back to him, smiling. "Um…consider it a done deal." Then she swiveled the chair so they faced the front of the shop. Ms. Van Hendler waved at them from the other side of the window.

"Mark my words, sugar, before the sun goes down to-night the whole county's going to know Virginia Boca gave Shaun Buchanan a really bad haircut in exchange for a re-ally good kiss. I hope you're prepared to find yourself at the center of another local scandal."

He smiled and lowered his mouth to hers, stopping just before their lips touched. "One kiss hardly qualifies as a scandal. Let's give 'em something to talk about."

Epilogue

Shaun stood at the front of a crowd of people, with Mendelssohn ringing in his ears, and watched Melody Merritt-Bradley bounce her newborn on her hip. Tyler Longfoot stood next to him, his attention locked on Ellie Longfoot positioned beside Melody in a similar rose-colored dress, cooing at the baby. Josh Bradley held the spot beside Tyler, and Shaun could feel the fire chief's enthrallment with his baby boy from this far away. Would he be that far gone over his own kid someday?

Before he could give the question much thought, the congregation of Bluelick Baptist stood and turned to face the other end of the aisle. An angel in white stood there, next to a man Shaun recognized as Mr. Boca, and somebody sucked all the oxygen out of the room.

He scanned the front pews and wished his father could have been there, but the white collar prison where Tom owed another eighteen months didn't allow for weekend weddings. His mother, however, waved from the first pew and hugged her husband's arm. All good there.

His attention drifted back to the aisle, where Virginia and her father drew near. She looked so perfect and remote beneath the filmy white veil, his head got a bit light. A hand landed on his shoulder, squeezed, and he realized Tyler had read his mind. Not all that surprising, considering Tyler had been in Shaun's shoes not too long ago. Still, he appreciated the solidarity.

A long wolf whistle sounded from somewhere in the line of men to his left. The congregation giggled at Junior's outburst, and the last bit of fog cleared from his head. He concentrated on Virginia, who stepped into the empty spot beside him in front of the altar.

Reverend Carlson asked, "Who gives this woman away?"

Mr. Boca murmured, "Her mother and I," kissed his daughter, and retreated to the front pew beside a suntanned, fifty-something version of Ginny.

He turned to the woman standing beside him. She still looked untouchable in her white dress and veil, but sparkling green eyes met his and she winked. His lips wanted to curve and he schooled them into a serious line. He dropped his eyes to the bouquet she held in front of her. A cascade of white flowers tumbled over her hands, but a dark spot in the opulence caught his eye. He looked closer, and realized she'd tucked a blush brush into the bouquet. He glanced up to her face and caught her sly smile and raised brow.

"I do," he said, cutting off Reverend Carlson's monologue.

"I'm sorry, Chief Buchanan. What did you say?"

He cleared his throat and spoke up. "I said I do. What do

you say, Virginia? Do you take me, too?"

She pushed the veil away from her face and smiled up at him. "I do," she replied, her husky voice strong and steady.

Reverend Carlson scrambled to get on the same page. "All right then. With the power vested in me by the state and the church, I now pronounce you husband and wife. You may kiss the bride."

"Brace yourself, sweet Virginia."

Her fingers brushed the hair at the nape of his neck. "Don't let the white dress fool you, sugar. I'm no virgin."

"You are, by one important measure."

Her brows drew together. "How do you figure?"

"You're spending your first night as a married woman with me. You going to kiss me, Mayor Boca, right here in plain sight of God and everyone?"

She came up on her tiptoes and claimed his lips. "Hell yes," she said against his mouth. "I have nothing to hide."

Acknowledgments

Let's kick things off with a huge thank you to Sue Winegardner and Heather Howland, as always, for whipping this story into shape and never laughing in my face. I can only imagine what happens behind my back, but I'm not going to question the magic.

To Liz Pelletier for adding your magic to the mix.

To Katie Clapsadl for pointing out, "Yes, you do have a newsletter sign up on your website," and not concluding the observation with, "you dumbass." I'm a lost cause, but I sincerely appreciate your efforts.

To Danielle Gorman. With your wizardry I may actually send out a newsletter someday.

To Robin Bielman for all the coffee, commiseration, celebrations, and for letting me turn our writing date into a movie date to see *Gone Girl*, and then trying to explain it to me.

To Hayson Manning for all the long-distance drinking,

commiserating, celebrating, and, of course, the Pornhub search tips.

To Maggie Kelley for your unflinching support, even when faced with the zebra dress.

To the lovely ladies (and manly men) of the Los Angeles Romance Authors.

To the readers! I hope you enjoyed the sexy adventures of Ginny and Shaun. Also, apparently I've got this newsletter you can sign up for….

To my family and friends. I trust you have signed up for my newsletter.

About the Author

USA TODAY bestselling author Samanthe Beck lives in Malibu, California, with her husband, their son, Kitty the furry Ninja, and Bebe the trash talkin' Chihuahua. When not writing fun and sexy contemporary romance, or napping on her beach towel with her face snuggled to her Kindle, she searches for the perfect ten dollar wine to pair with Lunchables.

Connect with Sam via Facebook, Twitter, or through her website at www.samanthebeck.com to check her progress on that never-ending quest, or to get the latest on her upcoming Brazens!

Made in the USA
Charleston, SC
06 February 2016